Spirits, Spells, and Storytelling:

13 Days of Hallows the Old Mermaids Way

Also by Kim Antieau

Old Mermaids Books
The Blue Tail • Church of the Old Mermaids
The First Book of Old Mermaids Tales • The Fish Wife
Magic, Myth, and Merrymaking: 13 Days of Yuletide the Old Mermaids Way
An Old Mermaid Journal • The Old Mermaids Book of Days and Nights
The Old Mermaids Book of Days and Nights: A Year and a Day Journal
The Old Mermaids Mystery School • The Old Mermaids Oracle
The Old Mermaids Wisdom Cards

Other Novels
Broken Moon • Butch • Coyote Cowgirl • Deathmark
The Desert Siren • Her Frozen Wild • The Gaia Websters
Jewelweed Station • The Jigsaw Woman • Killing Beauty
Mercy, Unbound • The Monster's Daughter • Queendom: Feast of the Saints •
The Rift • Ruby's Imagine • Swans in Winter • Whackadoodle Times
Whackadoodle Times Two • Whackadoodle Times Three
Whackadoodle Times Galore

Other Nonfiction
Answering the Creative Call • Certified: Learning to Repair Myself and the
World in the Emerald City • Counting on Wildflowers: An Entanglement
MommaEarth Goddess Runes • The Salmon Mysteries: a Reimagining of the
Eleusinian Mysteries • Under the Tucson Moon: Nine Winters in the Sonoran
Desert

SPIRITS, SPELLS, AND STORYTELLING

13 Days of Hallows the Old Mermaids Way

Kim Antieau

Green Snake
PUBLISHING

Contents

Introduction

Spirits, Spells, and Storytelling

Welcome to *Spirits, Spells, and Storytelling: 13 Days of Hallows the Old Mermaids Way.* In these pages, you will find ideas to charm, inspire, and spook as you celebrate Halloween for 13 days from October 21 through November 2.

The Halloween season—or the season of the witch—has always been my favorite time of year. I grew up in the country in southeastern Michigan. In October, the weather was cool and crisp. Dry leaves crunched under our feet. The skies were often gray, making the light perpetually spooky. We ran through local cemeteries where our dead relatives rested and decomposed, and we looked for ghosts and any signs of hauntings everywhere. We watched scary movies and anticipated the night when we could dress up as ghosts and ghouls and walk around in the nearly freezing cold in a nearby subdivision begging for candy. It was absolutely fantastic.

Even though Halloween, All Saints' Day, and All Souls' Day were a part of my parents' religion and/or a part of our culture, I didn't know much about the history of these holidays. It was only when I became an adult and explored the Pagan roots of so many holidays that I began to enjoy them again. For modern Pagans, Samhain (Halloween) is the final harvest celebration, and it's New Year's Eve. November 1 is the beginning of the ever turning Wheel of the Year. And Ancestor worship and honoring the dead is at the heart of all of these celebrations.

Ancestor worship is prevalent across the globe. Nearly every culture has some form of it. Everything I write about here has its roots in Old European Pagan rituals for honoring the dead, modern Halloween rituals, Day of the Dead (*Día de los Muertos*) rituals, and/or modern Pagan celebrations of Samhain, All Saints' Day, and All Souls' Day, all viewed through the eyes of the Old Mermaids.

How to Use This Book

I follow a similar pattern to the one in *Magic, Myth, and Merrymaking: 13 Days of Yuletide the Old Mermaids Way.* Each of the 13 days of Hallows has ideas for grounding, ceremony, rituals, poetry, charms, and honoring the ancestors. One of the 13 Old Mermaids from my novel *Church of the Old Mermaids* sponsors each day, if you will, and you can look to her for guidance or inspiration.

The main power days of these 13 days are October 30, 31, and November 1. You might want to flip ahead to those days and read up on them so you can plan your meals and/or ceremonies ahead of time. But here's a bit about those days in a nutshell.

Halloween, Samhain, Reign of the Cailleach, All Souls' Day, All Saints' Day, and Día de los Muertos (or Day of the Dead) are celebrated in a variety of ways on a variety of days depending on the culture.

Halloween is October 31st, and it is a popular holiday celebrated here in the United States by people dressing up in costumes, often frightening costumes, and with children going from house to house trick or treating. Mostly no tricking goes on; people give the children candy willingly. People carve out pumpkins and put lights inside. Sometimes people tell scary stories to each other.

Samhain is a Celtic holiday, generally, and is now considered a modern Pagan holiday that marks the end of the harvests for the year, marks the end of the year, and is a day to honor the dead. Often celebrations include a feast. Sometimes people have a Dumb Supper in honor of the dead. Other times, an empty chair is left at the table where the dead are served a meal along with the living around the table.

The veil is considered the thinnest on this day, so often various types of divinations are performed. Families construct altars to honor the beloved ancestors.

On November 1, the reign of The Cailleach begins. This powerful crone goddess rules the next six months of the year.

Catholics celebrate All Saints' Day on November 1 and All Souls' Day on November 2, but I won't be talking about these holidays from a Catholic point of view. They are essentially also holidays to show reverence for the dead and were most likely put into place at this time of year to usurp pagan holidays. I will note that November 2 is the day that Catholics often visited the graves of their relatives.

Día de los Muertos is observed primarily on November 1 and 2, although I've seen celebrations begin on October 31. This holiday is primarily celebrated in Mexico and in places in the United States. This is the time of the year when the dead return, so families do whatever they can to make them feel welcome. Many families create an altar (*ofrenda*) to honor the dead. In various places, people dress up, have parades and parties, sing and dance, and make offerings to their dead family members

Who Are the Ancestors?

The ancestors are our dead relations and loved ones. We share stardust—or the elements—with all the flora and fauna on this planet. So the plants and animals living (and dead) are all our relations, too.

Who Are the Old Mermaids?

The Old Mermaids began as characters in my novel *Church of the Old Mermaids.* In the book, their lives in the Old Sea ended when they washed ashore onto the New Desert where they "exchanged their finware for skinware." They had to learn not only how to survive but how to thrive in this new land.

They listened to the land and all their different kinds of neighbors, and they figured out how to live and celebrate every day as best they could. They did not venerate their ancestors the way their human neighbors did, but they had their own ways, and they incorporated those ways into what they learned.

Since I wrote *Church of the Old Mermaids,* the 13 Old Mermaids have become more than just characters in a book. I often ask myself, "What would the Old Mermaids do?" They have travails, yet they try to spread beauty in the world, in all the meanings of that word.

The Old Mermaids are realists, they don't hide their heads in the sand, and they help out their community. They are dreamers, magic-makers, artists, carpenters, seamstresses, faeries, and more. They don't judge, and they don't adhere to dogma. They look to Nature for answers. They love being alive and in the presence of their sister mermaids.

For each day of the *13 Days of Hallows the Old Mermaids Way,* I will have something you can read and some things you can do if you like. It is up to you. Each section begins with the name of a particular Old Mermaid from *Church of the Old Mermaids*. Think of her as a kind of "sponsor" for each day. She has wisdom, a suggestion, and gifts for you. It's up to you to accept them or not.

Day One:

Sister Sheila Na Giggles Mermaid

October 21

Sister Sheila Na Giggles Mermaid brings to mind the stone
carvings of Sheela Na Gigs in churches all across Western Europe.
She is usually depicted as an elderly or skeletal female figure
holding open her vagina. Perhaps our Sister Sheila Na Giggles
Mermaid was named after this ancient crone goddess. They seem

to share a similar worldview: This is what life is; don't hide from it.

Sister Sheila Na Giggles Mermaid brings this to you on this first day:

Suggestion: Get the starfish outta your eyes, sister.

Mystery: Be here now.

Gift: Guts!

Goddesses

The Irish Sheela Na Gigs are often associated with the great goddess Cailleach who is the dark mother, the crone or hag-goddess, goddess of the harvest. (It is pronounced "cal yuck.") The Cailleach rules this time of year. She is as unexplainable as she is dangerous. Think of her as our most ancient ancestor. It is said she shifts into her human form on Samhain and stays that way until May 1. Then Brigid comes out and replaces her, if you will, and rules the six months of light.

The Cailleach is the land, and she creates the land. In one story about her, mountains rise from boulders that drop from her apron as she strides across the land. When we honor the land, we are honoring her. In the time of honoring the ancestors, she is our primal ancestor.

Although she is often called a Celtic goddess or incarnation, she was part of the folklore of the region before the Celts arrived. Apparently she was so formidable, powerful, and influential that her stories then became part of Celtic folklore. Patricia Monaghan writes this about The Cailleach, "She represents all those aspects of life we must honor because we cannot avoid or deny them."

Yes.

Protection

This is the time of the year when the veils are thin. Or it may be the time of the year when the Good Friends have moved the veils aside so that they may travel from here to there and back again. It is a Mysterious Time, so who knows what can and will happen for certain? In any case, these can be dangerous times when the spirits may be drawn to us or we to them. It is important to stay grounded in this place in this now even if you decide you want to commune or communicate with the dear departed. It is important to keep yourself protected.

If you have your own grounding exercise, you can use that, of course. My favorite grounding exercise is to imagine roots growing out of the bottoms of my feet. These roots go through the floor and into the ground and then down deep, deep, deep until the roots reach the molten core of the earth. The roots drop right to the liquid and touch it. They are not burned. Instead, healing energy flows up my roots, up and up, until the healing energy flows into my legs and travels up my entire body and comes out the top of my head. At this point, if you are doing this exercise, you might raise yours arms and reach for the sky. The healing energy flows up and up and up until you are connected to the whole cosmos by this beam of healing energy that links everything together. When you feel the process has finished, let the energy flow down, go through your body and back down into the ground again. Stand or sit still for a moment, and then you are ready to greet the day.

Cauldron Bubble: What's to Eat or Drink?

Today is a time to honor the Sheela Na Gig and The Cailleach.

Their existence is ancient. They are of the body and the land.

Honor yourself and The Cailleach by cooking a rooted vegetable

stew. Most root vegetables are associated with winter. They have

grown up in the dark while being nourished from above.

Metaphorically at least, they represent darkness and survival.

If you don't want to cook, eat a carrot or some other root

vegetable. Imagine the nourishing darkness you are eating. It does a body good.

Dreams are Made of This

Dreams can be important ways to connect with ourselves and our ancestors. Before you go to sleep tonight, ask for a dream from an ancestor. Make certain you are grounded and feel connected to this world before making the request.

For now, leave the request vague: "I ask for a dream from an ancestor."

If you have a lot of nightmares normally, you might qualify the request by saying something like, "I would like a healing dream from an ancestor."

Keep a notebook and pen by the bed so you can immediately write down the dream upon awakening.

Altering the Altar

During these 13 days, I will suggest several ideas for altars. You can create one big altar that you add to during the 13 days or you can create several different altars during this process. If you already have an altar dedicated to the ancestors, you can add to it. Use this as an opportunity to redo your altar or create a whole new one. You choose.

Today decide if you want to make an altar dedicated

completely to The Cailleach or if you want to find one piece to honor and represent her to put on a larger altar.

Walk around your land or a park or your house, thinking about The Cailleach. She is formidable. Unapproachable. She is Nature, raw and real. See if a stone calls to you. Not a pebble, not a huge boulder. See if a fist-sized rock wants to go home with you. If it does, go to it and ask permission. Tell it what you want it for: either to honor and represent The Cailleach or as part of a whole altar dedicated to her. Before you pick it up—if it has given you permission—make certain you aren't disturbing any habitat if you remove it. If you are, go onto to the next rock that might be calling out to you. If you are dedicating an entire altar to The Cailleach, gather several fist-sized rocks. Carry them in the lap of your apron if you can and mark in your mind (or on paper) where you got the stones because you are going to bring them back when you're finished.

Some of you probably do not talk to rocks or trees or bees and/or fleas, and you're wondering how to ask a rock for permission. First, make certain you are grounded before the walk. Then set your intention: "I am creating an altar for The Cailleach. Who would like to go home with me?" And then walk with intention while paying attention. What catches your eye? If a rock is suddenly noticeable to you, it might be the rock—or one of the rocks. Go over and talk to it. You don't have to talk out loud, of course. Just carry on a conversation in your head and see what happens. Don't drive yourself crazy with any of this. It's supposed to be fun.

Once you have your rock or rocks, take them home. Get them ready for the altar in any way you choose. I've studied with many teachers from any different cultures, and all of them purify objects in some way when bringing those objects into a new space or place or when using them for something new. Each culture has a name for it, and they have different and similar ways to cleanse or purify. If you already have a way to prepare items for the altar, please feel free to use it.

I use different cleansing methods for different things. If I'm bringing something from Nature into the house, I make certain I am not bringing any critters in with it. For a rock, I would run it under the hose while whispering to it, saying a prayer of intention.

For instance: "I bring this stone into this new space for the purpose of honoring The Cailleach. I intend no harm and may it cause no harm. I will return it to (wherever it came from) when it is time. Blessed be." You can rhyme, if you like. Enchantments and prayers seem more powerful to me when they rhyme. They feel like songs the Universe truly hears. Afterward, I either bring the object into the house or I put it on the ground near the door overnight.

Many people cleanse by burning something and running the object through the flames or smoke. I do that if someone else has owned the object or if it's been sitting in a warehouse somewhere. I am very careful about using fire, though. I live in the West where things burn very easily. I try to use local plant material to burn like juniper which is something my Irish ancestors would have done. Again, I ask permission of the plant to be used in this way. I'm very intentional and careful about where the ashes, embers, and used matchsticks go.

When you feel the rock is ready to go indoors—if that's where you intend to put the altar—take it inside and place it intentionally with a simple prayer. "I honor you, Cailleach, and this dark time." If you have several rocks, put them in a circle or pile while stating your intention for this space. "I honor you, great Cailleach. May we be strong and healthy through this long winter."

There! You have honored The Cailleach.

Honoring the Ancestors

Today you have honored our most ancient ancestor (The Cailleach) by putting a stone on the altar in her honor.

Spooky is as Spooky Does

Remember this ghost craft from when you were a child? Get two tissues (Kleenexes). Crush one up into a ball. Then put the other tissue over it, and tie this second tissue around the balled up one so that it creates the ghost's head. Tie with dental floss, twine, or ribbon: whatever you have on hand. The rest of the second tissue hangs from the head as the ghost's body. Draw eyes, a nose, and a mouth on the ghost head. Put these all over your house to give yourself a grin.

Your tissue ghosts can also represent The Cailleach if you like, as long as they are created respectfully. (One wants to be careful around such power.) Her name may have been a title and it may have meant "the veiled one." Perhaps she is veiled to hide her human appearance as she embodies The Cailleach ceremoniously, like the Pythia after she inhales the vapors at Delphi.

Mostly, have fun. Children love this craft.

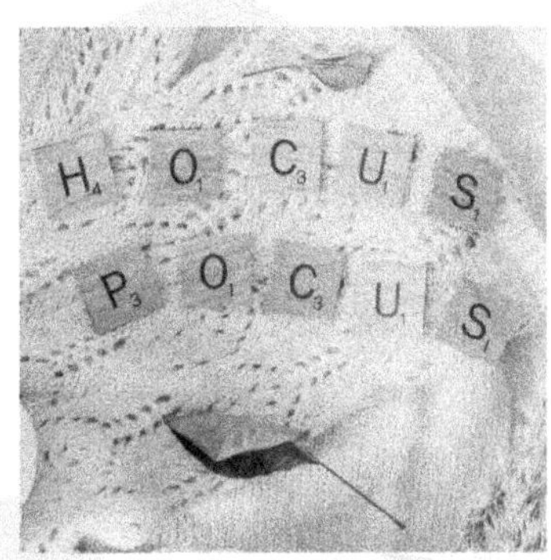

Charmed, I'm Sure

Charms can be spells or chants or enchantments. A spell is just a recipe for food or protection or healing. It is a way of singing to the Universe or with the Universe. A chant is a song; an enchantment is literally to sing. If you think of magic as the energy of the Universe, as the flow of the Universe, charms/chants/spells/enchantments are a way of helping you step onto that flow: or flow with the go. They are a way of helping you and the Universe understand each other.

This is rewritten from a protection prayer from the Carmina Gadelica. Where I've written Mother, you can use whatever name you wish. They used "thou," which I like, but I've substituted Mother, meaning the mother of the world.

Protection Prayer

Mother, my soul's Healer,
Keep me at even,
When all feels lost.
Keep me at morning,
When I cannot stand.
Keep me at noon,
When I am flailing.
On rough course faring,
Help and safeguard
My means this night
And every day and night.
I am tired, astray, and stumbling.
Shield me, Mother, from lies and apathy.
Shield me, Mother, from all that takes me from thou.

Samhain Symbols

Cats are probably associated with Halloween because they were considered familiars of witches and sorcerers. During the Inquisition, cats were often tortured and then burned alongside "their witches." The Inquisitors feared witches regularly shape-shifted into cats, especially black cats. During the Salem witch trails, the accused sometimes confessed that cats talked to them or that other people changed into cats.

In parts of Western Europe—especially in France—cat-burning was a form of entertainment for a time. Although I wasn't able to find out definitively why this happened, it could have been because they believed the devil shapeshifted into a cat now and again.

Cats have long been part of the stories of many goddesses. They were considered sacred to the Egyptians. Cats were depicted pulling the chariot of the Norse Goddess Freya. Some scholars believe that the cat was a favorite of The Cailleach.

Tales Told

"The Cailleach made that mountain over there," the Witch of Coyote Hill said, pointing.

It was pitch black night. None of the Old Mermaids could see a thing except the stars above.

"She had a boulder all wrapped up in her apron to take home and decorate her yard," the Witch said. "So I heard. Then someone said something she didn't like, and she just dropped that boulder where it was. Not sure how many villages she wiped out. Maybe some. Maybe none."

"Oh my," Sissy Maggie said. "That doesn't sound good."

"Good or bad," the Witch said, "you gotta be careful talking about her or telling stories about her. I mean, what if I got a detail wrong? She might be striding over us right this second with a boulder about to drop from her apron."

"What does she look like?" Sister DeeDee Lightful Mermaid asked. "Would we know her if we saw her?"

"Of course," the Witch said. "I heard she has one eye, white hair, and blue skin. Blue like the coldest night blue."

"I bet she looks like the mountain," Sister Ursula Divine Mermaid said.

"Or the night sky," Mother Star Stupendous Mermaid suggested.

"I imagine she knows everything," Sister Sheila Na Giggles Mermaid said.

"Shhh," the Witch said. "I think I hear her outside."

"I don't hear anything," Sister Sheila Na Giggles Mermaid whispered. "Except the blinking of one eye."

Day Two:

Sister DeeDee Lightful Mermaid

October 22

Sister DeeDee Lightful Mermaid urges us to be full of ourselves.

Just as Sister Sheila Na Giggles Mermaid suggests we face

reality, Sister DeeDee Lightful Mermaid suggests we face

ourselves and be full of our true selves. At the Temple of Delphi

where the Pythia famously foretold the future, students were urged to "know thyself." It is important during these 13 days—especially when the veil between worlds is thin—to be grounded and full of ourselves.

Sister DeeDee Lightful Mermaid brings these to the day:

Suggestion: Step lightly. Dance hard. Eat your vegetables.

Mystery: Be full of yourself.

Gift: Joy.

Goddesses

In my mind, Sister DeeDee Lightful Mermaid is associated with the Syrian goddess Atargatis and the Japanese goddess Amaterasu. Atargatis is one of the first known goddesses, and she was part fish. Amaterasu is a sun goddess of the Shinto religion. My knowledge of her is scant compared with those who cherish her as the Great Divinity Illuminating Heaven. The bare bones of her story is that she didn't trust her brother, so she retreated from the world, hiding her light in her Sky-Rock-Cave and throwing the world into darkness. She would not come out. Finally the goddess Uzume—reminiscent of Baubo in the Demeter story—began dancing and then doing a striptease outside the cave. Amaterasu was curious about the noise and laughter happening without her so she opened her cave door slightly. The other divinities had put a mirror right outside her door. Amaterasu looked upon herself and was dazzled by her light and beauty. The other divinities yanked the door open and kept it open. With Amaterasu's light shining, the world returned to normal.

Protection

Send roots down in the ground first thing in the morning. Then imagine that the Old Mermaids have spun you a magic protective suit. They put it on you, and it fits perfectly. You can't feel it. You don't have to energize it. You don't have to do anything. It doesn't hold anything in or anything out. Instead it transforms: Anything energetic that could harm you is rendered harmless. You are now powered up, protected, and energized.

Cauldron Bubble: What's to Eat or Drink?

On this second day, we celebrate ourselves and know ourselves.

All food is created by the sun, essentially. When we eat, we are

eating the sun. In honor of the sun goddess Amaterasu, eat the

sunniest food you can find. You choose!

Dreams are Made of This

Last night you asked for a dream from your ancestor. If you got one, did you understand it? If not, try "day-dreaming." This is a method I use to go back into a dream. Find a quiet place, take some deep breaths, close your eyes, and remember your dream. Then imagine yourself in the dream now and continue the dream. Let it unfold naturally, and feel free to ask questions of anyone in the dream. In this case, you might say, "I didn't understand the dream. Can you tell me specifically what your message is?" You can use this method to go back into any dream, even if you did understand the message.

If you didn't get a dream, don't worry. You are incubating dreams from your ancestors now. It may take some time. Try again tonight. Whether you had a dream or not, ask for a dream from an ancestor again. Don't ask for a particular ancestor to come to you in the dream. However, if you need help with a particular issue, ask for that help. "I am having trouble with money. Could an ancestor give me a helpful dream, please?" Or something along those lines. Remember to make certain you are grounded in this time and place before making the request.

Altering the Altar

Add a mirror to the altar. It can be a hand mirror, a compact, or any kind of small mirror. Cleanse it before you put it on the altar. Tell the cosmos, your ancestors, and yourself why you want the mirror on the altar: "I add this mirror with the intention of knowing myself and seeing the truth."

Honoring the Ancestors

We will continue to build the altar/altars during the 13 days, and that will be the main way of honoring our ancestors. Today you can start collecting photos or objects that represent your beloved dead.

Spooky is as Spooky Does

Scrying is a way of looking into the future and / or getting help from beyond the veil. Scrying is usually defined as divination using a mirror or some other reflective surface.

We have many stories in folklore and legends about the power of the mirror. Is it a completely other world behind the mirror? Is looking into a mirror a way to look directly beyond the veil to see the truth? For example, the Queen talks to a magic mirror in "Snow White and the Seven Dwarves." The goddess

Amaterasu looked into the mirror and realized how amazing she was, and the world was then saved. Mermaids are often depicted holding a mirror.

Some people purchase or make a black mirror to use for scrying. However, you can use any kind of reflective surface. It seems to work better if it's a dark reflective surface with water in it, like a cauldron, black pot, or a cast iron pot or pan.

One way of mirror divination is to sit in front of one in the darkness. Have one candle lit near the mirror. Make certain you've grounded and protected yourself. It's good to have on your Old Mermaid Suit. Then look into the mirror and chant. (See the chant in the next section or make up your own.)

Let your vision go fuzzy as you gaze into the mirror. Look beyond yourself into the darkness. What do you see? Does the darkness take on any kind of shape? A rabbit? A mountain? It's like looking at the clouds. Interpret what you see like you would

a dream or pulling a tarot card: What does it mean to *you*?

By the way, this can be a little spooky. Do it if you dare.

When you are finished, thank the Spirits for any messages. Make

certain you are fully grounded. Respectfully put out the flame of

the candle, and wash your hands under cold water.

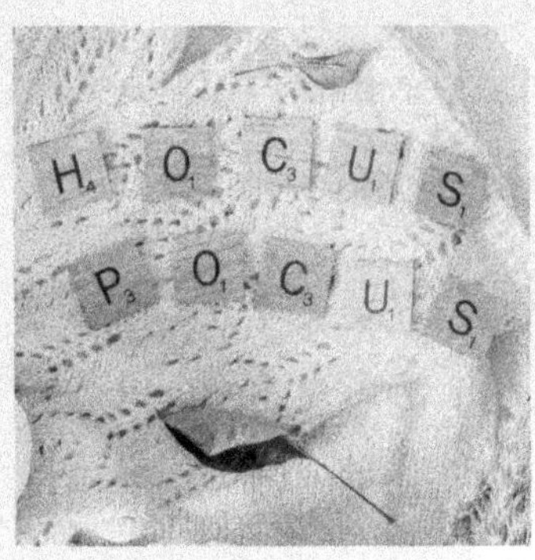

Charmed, I'm Sure

When working at this time of year when the veils are thin, when almost anything can become a portal, it is always good to keep yourself grounded and protected especially before calling on our ancestors for advice or help. The following is a chant you can use to honor and call upon the elements. I've used it for decades, so it has some resonance. I added lines to the end that you can use if you are doing any scrying. Rewrite it and make it your own:

Charm to Honor and Call the Elements

I call upon the compassionate spirits of the east and the air:

Help me to dare.

I call upon the compassionate spirits of the south and the fire:

Help with my desire.

I call upon the compassionate spirits of the west and the water:

Help me be a healed and healing daughter/son.

I call upon the compassionate spirits of the north and the earth:

Help with my rebirth here and now in this body.

Please protect all of me

As you let me see.

Please protect all of me

As you let me see.

Please protect all of me

As you let me see

What message you have for me.

Samhain Symbols

The mirror was once more of a symbol of Halloween than it is now. Through them, people contacted the "spirits" who could tell them the future. A hundred years ago or more at midnight on Halloween, girls and women would sit in front of the mirror with only one candle burning while eating an apple and ask the mirror for a vision of their future husband. If the spirits were obliging, a vision of their husband would appear in the mirror.

Tales Told

One year, a few of the Old Mermaids were missing the Old Sea. Especially Sister DeeDee Lightful Mermaid. Her tears for all they had lost were constant. It was the time of the year after the monsoons, after much of the desert had been flooded by a particularly rainy summer. And the moon was so full and bright at night for a few days that the Old Mermaids wondered if it was full of something besides reflected sunlight.

On one of these nights when most of the Old Mermaids

slept, the Witch of Coyote Hill told Sister DeeDee Lightful Mermaid and Sister Lyra Musica Mermaid, "I can show you where the Old Sea and all you knew still lives. But we must go now, and you can't say a word on the way there."

"But what of our sister mermaids?" Sister Lyra Musica Mermaid asked. "They would want to go too."

"I saw no tears on their cheeks tonight," the Witch of Coyote Hill said. "It is now or it is never."

So the two Old Mermaids followed the Witch out into the brightest night they had ever seen.

"When did the Moon get so big?" Sister DeeDee Lightful Mermaid asked. "We will have to show Sissy Maggie when we return."

The Witch dropped into the wash, and the Old Ems walked behind her. The hackberry and acacia trees reached out skeletal branches to them. The Witch hummed as she walked. Although as Sister DeeDee Lightful Mermaid watched, it seemed the Witch was floating as she walked. She looked down. Maybe they were floating, too.

Ahhh. The Witch was weaving an enchantment.

Perhaps.

They walked out of the wash and followed the Witch into the desert. Somehow they were in the Mountains. The Old Ems held hands. The Witch climbed up onto a rock and then disappeared. The Old Ems followed her. She was standing next to a small pool in a rock cropping that reflected the moon above.

The Witch said, "This was created from all your tears. Beneath this surface is the Old Sea and all you left behind. You only have to see it."

The Old Mermaids knelt by the pool. They put their hands on the stone around it and leaned forward slightly. They could see their own reflections.

"I see Sister DeeDee Lightful Mermaid," Sister Lyra Musica Mermaid said.

"And I see Sister Lyra," Sister DeeDee Lightful Mermaid said.

"Look deeper," the Witch said.

Sister DeeDee Lightful Mermaid breathed deeply, and she continued to gaze. After a few moments, her vision blurred. Or maybe it cleared. Ahhh. She saw the Old Old Mermaids lounging somewhere near a distant shore. Their gorgeous tails flashed in the moonlight of a half moon. They were laughing. And talking. Sister DeeDee Lightful Mermaid could hear them but not understand them. There was Grand Mother Yemaya Mermaid, her two blue-green tails moving her through the darkness. And wait, there she was—Sister DeeDee Lightful Mermaid—with Grand Mother. She was laughing, too; she was filled with joy, and Sister Bea Wilder Mermaid was waving to her from nearby. The world looked perfect. Yes, that was where she wanted to be. Not in this dry nearly waterless place where joy was difficult to come by. They were so close. If she put out her hand, she knew she could touch them.

So Sister DeeDee Lightful Mermaid put her hand into the water. The surface broke and she could no longer see. She reached down farther, deeper; she was about to go all the way into the pool; something touched her fingers, grabbed her.

Sister Lyra Musica Mermaid said, "It's the past, Sister DeeDee. That's not us. That's what we were."

The fingers on the other side pulled on her. She could feel herself slipping, wanting to go with whoever held her hand.

"If you go, the person you are now will never exist," the Witch said.

"I was more fun then," Sister DeeDee Lightful Mermaid

said. "Everything was possible. Now, it feels like nothing is possible."

Sister Lyra Musica Mermaid stood and held her hand out to Sister DeeDee Lightful Mermaid. "Everything is possible. It's just different. And sometimes sadder."

Sister DeeDee Lightful Mermaid closed her eyes. She could just let herself go into the water. Back to the Old Sea again.

"I'm not what I used to be," Sister DeeDee Lightful Mermaid said.

"And you never will be," Sister Lyra Musica Mermaid said, "even if you leave us now."

The pull on her hand in the water became more insistent.

"You get to decide if you still want to live now," the Witch said, "with the grief. With the changes. The past only holds the dead."

The Witch held Sister Lyra's other hand.

Sister DeeDee Lightful Mermaid looked back at the pool. She could see the blue hand that held hers. Could see flashes of tails in the water. She looked back up at Sister Lyra Musica Mermaid.

"Leave your tears behind for tonight," Sister Lyra Musica Mermaid said. "Come home with me. They are all dreaming of you in the here and now."

Sister DeeDee Lightful Mermaid grabbed Sister Lyra Musica Mermaid's hand and let go of the blue hand in the water, let go of all that held her back, all that was calling her to end her time in the desert. Sister Lyra and the Witch pulled her to her feet. When she looked down again, the pool was gone.

Sister Lyra Musica Mermaid put her arm around Sister DeeDee Lightful Mermaid's waist.

"What a night," Sister Lyra said. "Have your ever seen a moon like this?"

"I never have," Sister DeeDee Lightful Mermaid said. "It's one for the ages."

And they walked back to the Old Mermaids Sanctuary together. Or maybe they floated on the Witch's enchantments.

Day Three:

Sister Bea Wilder Mermaid

October 23

Sister Bea Wilder Mermaid watches over this day. She wants you to bewilder and be wilder. Take a little walk on the wild side, as it were. During this time of year, everything feels wild, doesn't it? Unexpected and sometimes good scary. Dance to the sound of the dry leaves underfoot or the sound of the wind through the trees. Connect with the darkness all around.

Sister Bea Wilder Mermaid brings these to the day:

Suggestion: Things change. Get over it.

Mystery: Embrace the wild.

Gift: Ecstatic Dance.

Goddesses

For the 13 days of Hallows, this day belongs to the Maenads, the supposedly mad Greek women who followed the religion of Dionysus, the inebriated god of the wild. We know very little about the Maenads. They aren't goddesses but real women who somehow had their own religion and met together in the wilds to worship without male companions. We don't know how they worshipped, but male writers claimed they got drunk, tore wild animals limb from limb, and then drank their blood. And if a boy or man happened upon their frenzied worship, they would kill him, too.

Patricia Monaghan writes in *The Goddess Path* that Dionysus was connected to Ariadne (originally a Cretan goddess). She was his wife and the "chief Maenad." Monaghan says about the Maenads, "They were proto-feminists, striking back at the patriarchal religion by embracing a foreign and outlandish god." Dionysus wore women's clothes when they paraded through the streets, with him in the lead. "Or perhaps they were driven by a deep psychic need to embrace their own divine nature, which they realized in the ecstasy of their woodland rituals," Monaghan writes.

Some scholars believe the stories of the Maenads were based on flesh and blood mentally ill women who were left to roam the countryside by society, like dogs let loose to become feral. Others believe that Greek women were so repressed by the patriarchal society they lived in that it was natural that they would erupt into this kind of structured madness occasionally.

Still others say the Maenads were priestess-shamans, disguising their sacred work in stories of madness. They may have "worshipped" the male-god Dionysus the way African slaves who were kidnapped and brought to the United States worshipped Jesus and cloaked their spirits in the robes of Christian saints. These disguises protected them and their religion and allowed them a moderate semblance of freedom to pursue their spiritual beliefs in societies that did not allow true freedom. Free autonomous women worshiping an ancient goddess and performing her rites was not something the Greek patriarchy would have tolerated easily.

In her article "Medea and the Shaman Women of the Silk Road," Vicki Noble writes that the Maenads were part of an "unbroken lineage of ecstatic shaman women that can be documented from ancient to present times across vast geographical regions." She goes on to say, "From Tibetan Buddhist dakini practices . . . to 'tantric' traditions alive in India today we can see vestiges of this ancient female lineage that began in the Neolithic (if not earlier) and included priestesses of the Aegean Bronze and Iron Ages (called in Greek 'Maenads'), the shaman women of Central Asian tribes, and the cemetery-dwelling yoginis and wandering 'dakini-witches' of India and Tibet." Noble believes this lineage also includes the Valkyries, Banshee, the Tocharian mummies, and the witches murdered during the "Burning Times."

The Maenads performed ecstatic rites and shamanistic ceremonies. They drummed up their ecstasy in the forests. They took care of the bees and brewed mead from honey. These bee priestesses were called Melissa. The Melissa was a title given to someone who acted as a priestess, most often a priestess to Artemis or Demeter.

While we don't know their full herstory, these women seemed to have carved out a way to practice their ecstatic religious rites in a very patriarchal society. That is amazing.

Protection

Ground and center yourself by sending your roots into the earth and taking in the healing energy of the planet and connecting yourself to the sky as you've done previously. Put on the protection suit the Old Mermaids created for you. Then consider purifying and protecting yourself with smoke, water, salt, or crystals.

    If you use smoke, be very careful of what you burn, how you burn it, and how you dispose of it. It is best to use plants that have historically been used to purify like rosemary, juniper, or sage. Use plants you have grown yourself. Many of the bundles of white sage or palo santo that you buy at the store have been harvested unsustainably. Most cultures have used smoke to cleanse. Just do it mindfully with conversations with the plant. Once it has given you permission to harvest it and use it, light it carefully, and ask it to protect and purify. As you run the smoke around your body, imagine any cords and ties that bind dissolving.

That said, I rarely use smoke to cleanse. For one thing, it's smoke, and it's not good for our lungs. For another thing, we need to be so careful of anything catching fire where I live. If I've been having trouble with nightmares or I want to shake myself out of a downturn in my life, I will use smoke while standing in our screened-in porch (with a concrete floor).

You can use water and or salt or use them together by mixing the salt with the water. Sprinkle it on you while asking for purification and protection.

If you have crystals, you can use those. Run amethyst, clear crystal, or tourmaline over your body.

Remember, you do this not because you are dirty and need cleaning. Think of it as clearing the decks to prepare yourself for ceremony. Once finished, you are open, ready, and protected.

After the cleansing, call in the elements and directions for protection using the charm/chant from yesterday. Consider asking one or more of the Old Mermaids to join you in the ritual or ceremony.

Cauldron Bubble: What's to Eat or Drink?

Eat some wild food today. If there's anything in your environment that is safe to harvest and eat, do it. Berries? Dandelion? Again, know what you're doing. Don't ever harvest anything unless you are 100% certain what it is. If there isn't anything outside you can harvest, eat some berries from your freezer or fruit from anywhere. Imagine it in its natural state. Imagine it being harvested by a group of wild women. Imagine the Old Mermaids out in the desert gathering food. Can you see yourself there?

Dreams are Made of This

Have you had a significant dream from an ancestor yet? Maybe you have and don't realize it. An ancestor dream doesn't necessarily mean that they show up in the dream and tell you what to do. Maybe you get a message in your dream that you need to get more rest. That sounds like a message from an ancestor. If you want to know which ancestor, you can look around in the dream. Was there a sweater your favorite aunt wore in the dream? Was your grandfather's pipe in the ashtray?

Consider it could also be an ancestor you don't know or recognize. Try again tonight. Keep track of your dreams.

Altering the Altar

Find something that represents your wild ancestors, human and otherwise. Honor those women who fought against the patriarchy. Honor the Maenads if you wish by putting a drum on the altar.

Honoring the Ancestors

Do you have an ancestor that people didn't really understand? Someone who was good people but often the odd person out? Was she outcast? Did others make fun of him? Honor those people in your bloodline who didn't quite fit in. Even if you don't know of one, they existed. Hold them in your heart and thoughts. Thank them.

Spooky is as Spooky Does

The word maenad apparently means "to rave," although some definitions say it literally means "mad woman." Become a Mad Woman for a day, an hour, a few minutes. Take your drum or rattle into the woods or desert or wherever you live and dance. Become ecstatic. You will find delight in that.

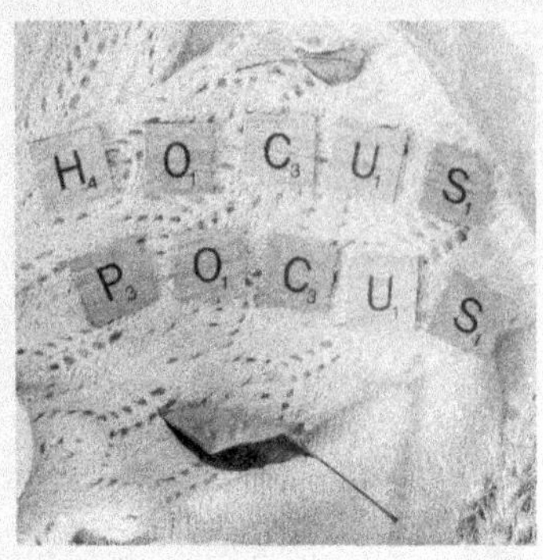

Charmed, I'm Sure

Here's a charm you can recite while out dancing in the wild:

Charm For Maenads

Maenad, maenad, maenad.

Say it ain't so bad.

Maenad, maenad, maenad.

Say it ain't so sad.

Let this patriarchy malarkey

Be a fad

Fading, fading, fading fast.

Now let our women's power last and last.

Samhain Symbols

Costumes and masks are associated with Halloween. According to many sources, this Halloween tradition began in 15th century Scotland, although there is some evidence that it began 2,000 years ago. Our European ancestors believed spirits roamed the Earth looking for souls to take back with them at this time of year. People put on masks and costumes to fool the spirits.

Some scholars believe that masks became popular because

Pagans had to hide who they were from the Inquisitors or mettlesome neighbors who might turn them in for dancing in the streets. Modern Pagans and others who practice Earth-based religions consider Halloween/Samhain as New Year's Eve and often dress in costumes to inhabit the essence of who they want to become in the new year.

Tales Told

"In another time and place, I was a little boy running through the woods in the mountains," the Witch of Coyote Hill said, "when I heard the Mad Women drumming and singing. I knew if they spotted me, they would tear me limb from limb and drink my blood. So I immediately turned away, scared to death, and bolted—only I tripped over a root and fell. Before I could get up, a woman dressed in forest finery stood over me. Leaves and flowers were stuck in her hair. Her eyes were like balls of fire. I whimpered. Then she said, 'We were rolling down the hill. You wanna join us?'

"'Are you going to tear me limb from limb and drink my blood?'

"Her eyes narrowed. She licked her lips. 'Naw. I don't like little boy blood. It stinks to high heaven. Come on!'

"She ran away from me calling out, 'we've got cookies' as she went. I couldn't resist cookies."

"Did they tear you from limb to limb?" Sister DeeDee Lightful Mermaid asked.

"Did they drink your blood?" Sister Bea Wilder Mermaid asked.

"No," the Witch said. "They gave me cookies and taught me how to drum. Nothing to see here. No horror. No madness. Happily ever after."

Day Four:

Sister Lyra Musica Mermaid

October 24

Sister Lyra Musica Mermaid encourages us to silence our fears so we can sing our siren songs even as detractors try to shut us up.

Sister Lyra Musica Mermaid brings these to the day:

Suggestion: Fear has no sisters, but I have many.

Mystery: Live Your Siren Song.

Gift: Stories.

Goddesses

Sister Lyra Musica Mermaid is connected to Artemis. (Some of you may remember the story of her and Mr. Hunter.) And her relationship with Artemis connects her with the Pythia, the Delphic priestess who predicted the future in ancient Greece.

Delos, Dodona, and Delphi in ancient Greek were places people traveled to seek the prophecies of the priestesses of the Earth Mother. According to Vicki Noble in her book *Shakti Woman*, "Delos belonged originally to Artemis and later was moved to Delphi, where it eventually belonged to the god Apollo, even though the priestess was still female and still had a snake—the famous python."

Delphi is a beautiful mysterious place. It throbs with wildness, up in the mountains with an amazing view of the countryside. It is easy to imagine it as a center to learning and prophecy. The motto at Delphi apparently was "know thyself." The priestesses were not goddesses but human women who may have trained to become the Pythia by inhaling fumes from the Earth itself. I love the idea of this place out in Nature where women could learn to be powerful, especially given how patriarchal the Greeks were.

Protection

Continue to send down roots, put on your Old Mermaids Suit,

call in the directions and elements, and purify yourself.

Cauldron Bubble: What's to Eat or Drink?

What is your favorite thing to eat when you gather with siblings?

Make it or buy it. If you don't have siblings, choose what you

want to eat. Sing a song before you eat, and then celebrate.

Dreams are Made of This

Have you gotten any dreams from the ancestors? If so, have you gone back into them? Have you "daydreamed" with them? Tonight dream with a crystal. Amethyst is a good dreaming stone. Make sure the stone is clean and willing to work with you. If you haven't already, cleanse the stone with smoke or water or put it on top of a rose quartz stone for a while.

Then meditate with it. Make certain you are centered and grounded and in your Old Mermaid power suit. Ask for protection and guidance, and then go to where your crystal came into existence. (Usually a cave somewhere.) Use your imagination. Once there, do a healing on the land. Leave an offering. Thank the crystal for coming into your life. Ask if it is willing to work with you. Then say your goodbyes to the land.

Come back into your room. Tell the stone what your intention is for the night: "Could you give me an ancestor dream with a clear message, please?" Then put the stone on the night table, under your bed, or under your pillow. See what happens!

Altering the Altar

In honor of Sister Lyra Musica Mermaid, add a small musical instrument or something that represents music to you. And/or place a bit of snake skin to honor the Pythia.

Honoring the Ancestors

Be intentional as you go through these 13 days. Think of your relatives, but also think of the flora and fauna on this planet that have helped you survive and thrive. Honor them, too.

Spooky is as Spooky Does

Become the Pythia. Go somewhere dark, sit on a stool, hang your head a bit, and see what comes to you. Ground, center, power up. Decide on what question you would like to explore. Macro or micro? About your life or the world? Don't try to control what comes into your mind. Say it out loud or write it down as it comes.

After you feel finished, write down what you remember if you haven't already. Read it later. Interpret it as you would a dream, not as an absolute truth. Have fun with it. That is the most important part of the process.

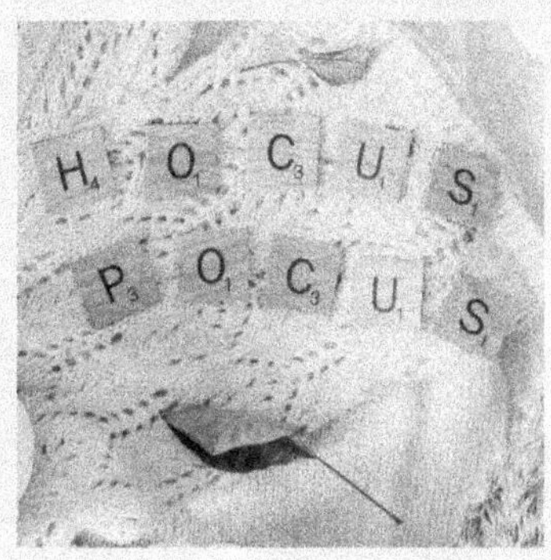

Charmed, I'm Sure

Say this three times for yourself or someone else who is going through challenging times:

Charm for Challenging Times

Your days have been rough.

Your nights have been tough.

Power of bear on you.

Speed of the gazelle on you.

Perspective of the eagle on you.

Good health of a thousand healthy people on you.

Good home, good health, good people.

Now your days and nights are bright and clear

And you have nothing left to fear

For you and all you hold dear.

Samhain Symbols

Why is candy associated with Halloween? Lots of people have lots of ideas of how it came to be: It was the Irish, the Catholics, the Americans! Or it was a good marketing job by candy companies.

Probably if I dug a little more and a little deeper I could come up with a good nuanced answer to this question. Instead, I will say that nowadays, many Pagans who celebrate Samhain and Halloween as New Year's Eve give out candy to children to start out their new year with sweetness. I love that tradition and figure I am following it every time I hand out candy to children on Hallows.

Tales Told

This story is based on a meeting between Sister Lyra Musica Mermaid and the Queen of the Night flower. It's from The Old Mermaids Wisdom Cards *guidebook, and I thought it is a perfect way to honor our flora ancestors. The Pythia may have been able to see into the future, but the Queen of the Night understands that the present is important.*

One year, Sister Lyra Musica Mermaid was out walking in the

desert. As often happens when faeries are afoot—even when one might be a faery—Sister Lyra Musica Mermaid got separated from the other Old Mermaids. She was left alone in the dark. In the desert. In the time of year when the rattlesnakes were out. And the mountain lions. Coyotes. She was an Old Mermaid: She didn't worry about such things. Except when she did.

Before this new life, she would have dived deep into the ocean and gotten away from any danger. At least, that was what she believed. Now she often felt herself sinking inward—almost as though she was getting smaller—so that nothing could touch her or hurt her again. Or maybe her heart was getting smaller because she didn't think she could take one more heartache.

Now, suddenly on this night, a woman in white was walking toward her in the desert. It wasn't that she was wearing white. It was as if she were a beautiful flower with a light at her center that made her a human-like lantern.

"Hello, Sister Lyra," the flower woman said as she held out her hand to Sister Lyra Musica Mermaid.

"Hello, Queen of the Night," the Old Mermaid said, taking the woman's hand in hers.

The Queen of the Night smiled. She led Sister Lyra Musica Mermaid around the pencil cholla, the teddy bear cholla, the mesquite trees, and creosote bushes to a clearing in the desert where several other Queens of the Night were dancing. They all looked different from each other yet were the same, too, dancing under the stars.

"Shall we dance?" the Queen of the Night asked Sister Lyra.

Sister Lyra Musica Mermaid said, "Of course."

And so Sister Lyra Musica Mermaid danced with this Queen and then all of the Queens of the Night until her feet were sore and the sky began to lighten.

"This was so much fun," Sister Lyra Musica Mermaid said. "I can't wait to do it again. I will miss you all so. Shall we meet next year at the same time?"

The Queen smiled. "You long for what was and you fear what will be."

"I want to always be this happy," Sister Lyra Musica Mermaid said.

The Queen laughed. "This here and now is what we have."

Sister Lyra Musica Mermaid smiled. "I know it's best to live in the present. But it was so awful when we lost the Old Sea. I miss it so much sometimes that it hurts."

"Then miss it," the Queen said. "And let it hurt. The hurt will subside. Or it won't. Things are not always easy. Yet beauty is lurking around somewhere most of the time. Open your heart to it all."

Sister Lyra Musica Mermaid closed her eyes for a moment and breathed deeply. Then she nodded, opened her eyes, and said, "I will do just that."

The other queens came and hugged and kissed Sister Lyra Musica Mermaid. Then they drifted away until all their lights were out of sight. Just then the Sun rose, and golden light streamed across the desert. Sister Lyra Musica Mermaid watched it for a time, and then she hurried home to the Old Mermaids

Sanctuary.

Day Five:

Sister Laughs A Lot Mermaid

October 25

Sister Laughs A Lot Mermaid brings us laughter and a good time wherever she goes. That is her profound gift to us all.

She offers these to the day:

Suggestion: She who laughs a lot laughs a lot.

Mystery: Cultivate Joy.

Gift: Laughter.

Goddesses

We've all heard of the banshee, a female spirit who shrieks before the death of a family member. Irish families were each supposed to have one. If you heard a woman keening in the distance, the sound would send shivers of fear up your spine—particularly if you were Irish. However, banshee is a corruption of the word *bean sidhe* (pronounced "banshee") which means woman of the mounds. The banshee—the bean sidhe—were fairy women. And before that, they were most likely goddesses like Aine, the

Banshee Queen. She most likely came to Ireland with the Tuatha
Dé Danann, the people of the goddess Danu, a race of people
said to occupy Ireland before it was Ireland. When they left, they
went into the mounds of Ireland. The fey are the descendants of
the Tuatha Dé Danann.

Protection

Continue what you've been doing for the last few days: Send roots down into the earth and put on the Old Mermaid suit. If you like, drop a gem or two in your pocket or around your neck. Ask the stones ahead of time if they'll help keep you safe if you haven't already asked or "charged" them. (Run water over them, leave them on the ground or in the moonlight. Talk to them.)

Cauldron Bubble: What's to Eat or Drink?

Honor the bean sidhe and Aine with a feast of potatoes and eggs: eggs for the sun and potatoes for the dark moon. Or create any other feast that you think would honor a fairy queen. Simple and splendid are the watch words.

Dreams are Made of This

Ask for a dream from your ancestors or from the fairy queen.
Don't ask about the future necessarily. Ask for help with a
problem here and now. Write the dream down first thing, and
then interpret it and follow the prescription—as long as it isn't
dangerous or hurtful. And remember, it's always your choice.

Altering the Altar

Put on your altar items that honor the banshee side of the bean sidhe and the fairy queen/goddess side: Something black or white for mourning and beautiful baubles for the fairy queen perhaps.

Honoring the Ancestors

Today you honor the bean sidhe, and that is honoring your ancestors. It is said that each family had their own bean sidhe to warn them and watch over them. Recognize that your family may have believed this or something similar. Imagine the chill they felt when they heard a scream in the night and wondered who was going to die. It took a lot of courage for so many of our ancestors to survive. Honor that.

Spooky is as Spooky Does

Go out to the crossroads and listen for the bean sidhe. Can you hear what she has to say beyond her grief? It's a grief of lost land and lost power and lost lives. Can you hear her wail? Can you hear her whisper? If you were a bean sidhe for your family, what truth would you keen? Feel free to wail. And then consider how to step into your power even as you grieve. How do we get past grieving for what has been lost?

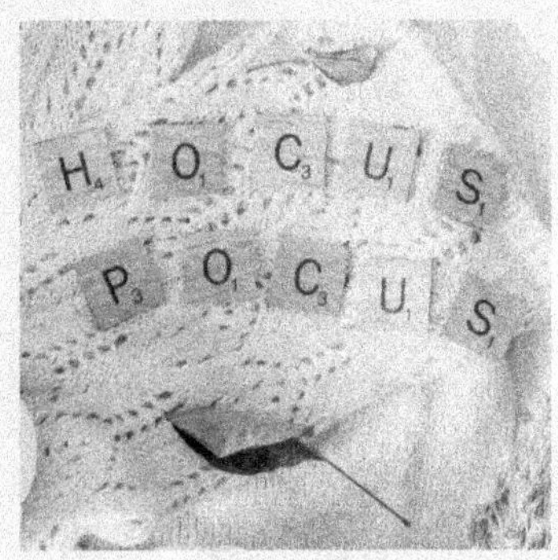

Charmed, I'm Sure

This is a rewriting of an old Serbo-Croatian charm.

Charm for Grief

When in the binding circle of grief:

May your heart find some healing relief

May your soul's pain be but brief

May your feet elude joy's cruel thief

May acceptance be your new motif

May your hand catch a falling leaf
Comfort in the arms of grief.

Samhain Symbols

No one is certain how jack o' lanterns came into existence although my friend Patricia Monaghan came up with some great research that may explain it a bit. She says that in Ireland "a light seen over bogs at night" was said to be a lantern carried by a doomed dead gambler. "His soul was too stained to enter heaven," but he had beat the devil at cards so he wouldn't have to go to hell. People hollowed-out turnips on Samhain and named them after him: Jack o' Lantern.

Another theory is that country folk used the vegetable lanterns when they were out in the woods celebrating. After a while, they started carving scary images to frighten away Nosy Nellies and inquisitors. When Europeans came to North America, they brought the vegetable lantern tradition with them, using pumpkins in place of turnips.

Some say that the light in the jack o' lantern—whatever vegetable it came in—has always meant one thing: Spirits are welcome here!

Tales Told

"One night I went out to the crossroads," the Witch of Coyote Hill told the Old Mermaids. "My Old Ma, the woman who taught me everything, told me I had to go out and meet Death before she comes to meet me. I didn't know what she meant, but I went out to the crossroads, that place where everything meets. I thought I might see the great goddess Trivia—she of the three roads—or Hecate. I stood in the darkness except for the light of the stars above me. I breathed in starlight and breathed out darkness, I breathed in starlight and breathed out darkness. After a while, I heard a howl. It was long and deep and pitiful, and I knew this howl was a death knell. Or was it a prediction of a death? Was it the banshee's cry?

"I stood in the darkness shivering and listening to the howl. Only it wasn't one howl but several. After a few moments, it stopped, and a coyote ran by me. I laughed at myself. What I was certain was a howl of death was only a coyote calling out for others of its kind.

"Later I heard a scream. I was certain it was the scream of someone dying brutally. When the sound stopped, an owl flew overhead. I laughed at myself.

"In fact every sound that frightened me that night was made by Nature. Yet for a long while, I could only hear them as if they were messages from another human being.

"And when night was just about to gray into daylight, a being completely covered in black and light came toward the crossroads. I could hear her breathing. It was like listening to the entire planet breathing. Her appearance was terrifying, although I cannot explain to you why. I had never seen blackness and light wrapped up together. I knew she was a bean sidhe, a fairy queen.

"'Whose death have you foretold?' I asked.

"She laughed. When she laughed, she breathed out darkness, and she breathed out light.

"'Everyone's.'

"My eyes widened.

"'Eventually,' she said. 'What question do you have?'

"'Why do we suffer?' I asked without a thought.

"She shrugged. 'I don't know.'

"'But aren't you a goddess? Aren't you supposed to know everything?'

"'Whatever I am, I do not know the answer to that question.'

"'Can I do anything to stop myself and others from suffering?'

"She sighed. 'Why would you want to stop?'

"'Why? Isn't it obvious? It hurts. It's painful.'

"'Those are all good reasons,' she said.

"'Why did you come here,' I asked, 'if you have no answers?'

"She cocked her head. 'Perhaps I came because I had a question for you.'

"'Me? What could I tell you that you don't already know?'

"'Why do you suffer?' she asked.

"'I-I don't know,' I said.

"She nodded. 'Then perhaps you are a goddess, too.'"

Day Six:

Sister Ursula Divine Mermaid

October 26

Sister Ursula Divine Mermaid encourages us to figure out how to be most at home in the world with our wild natural selves. She brings these to the day:

Suggestion: I am most at home where the wild things are.

Mystery: Be at home in the world.

Gift: Knowledge of wild things.

Goddesses

The name Ursula means bear, and Sister Ursula Divine Mermaid is related to the great Gaelic bear goddess, Artio. In fact, King Arthur may have gotten his name from Artio. We know little of the worship of the She-bear goddess except that she was seen as the goddess of wildlife and abundance. And it is possible people worshipped her for thousands of years. According to Barbara Walker, the worshippers of Artio further north from Ireland were the berserkers: those who wore bear skins and became fierce invincible warriors.

Our human relationship with bears is long and deep. Many of our ancestors believed they were related to the bear. Bears were seen as people. I wrote a novel about them (*Her Frozen Wild*) after years of very intense bear dreams.

Symbolically, bear is often seen as a healer or a healing presence as well as potential danger in our lives.

Protection

Ask bear if s/he will protect you. Agree to do something for her. Give money to an organization that protects bears. Dance a bear dance.

Cauldron Bubble: What's to Eat or Drink?

Eat some honey today. Imagine you are a bear just about to go into hibernation for winter. Would you eat anything else? Salmon, maybe.

Dreams are Made of This

Dream of bear. If you don't dream of bear, can you remember any other dreams you've had about bear over the years? What *did* they mean to you then? What *do* they mean to you now?

Altering the Altar

Put something on the altar that represents bear.

Honoring the Ancestors

Add something or some things to the altar that represent all the plants, animals, bacteria, and fungi that have gone extinct since you've been alive. We are in the midst of a Sixth Mass Extinction—the Holocene extinction—which is caused by human activity. Honor and mourn what has been lost.

Spooky is as Spooky Does

Be the bear. Embody the bear in whatever way you can. Bear dances still take place in Russia. In some villages, men and women and some children dress up in real bearskins and dance. It is extraordinary. And shamans in Siberia still do their version of the bear dance to embody bear spiritually and to honor the Bear Clan. I've had many dreams of bear, but the most amazing one was when I climbed a tree to get away, and I looked down and saw I had grizzly claws. It was quite a powerful feeling.

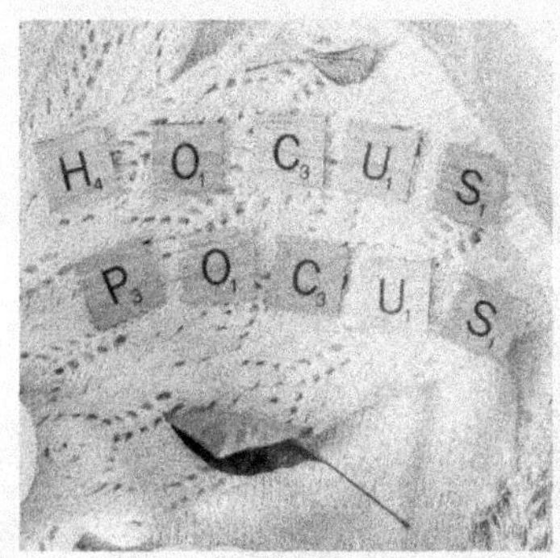

Charmed, I'm Sure

Before Siberian hunters killed a bear, they stood outside its cave and pleaded with it. They acknowledged it was their ancestor and called it Grandfather and apologized for killing it. Fortunately, we have no need to kill any bears, but we can still honor our connection with bears and bear spirit.

Charm to Honor Connection of Bear

Grandfather Bear, Grandmother Bear

Help me to dare

Grandfather Bear, Grandmother Bear

    Help me to care

Grandfather Bear, Grandmother Bear

    It is me, your child

Help me to always stay wild.

Grandfather Bear, Grandmother Bear

Tales Told

Just about this time of year one fall, one of the largest sunflowers in the Old Em garden bowed its head to signal it was ready to be harvested. Sister Ruby Rosarita Mermaid and Sister Ursula Divine Mermaid went to the sunflower, thanked it, then beheaded it.

They whispered thank yous to all the sunflowers ever grown. They broke the head in two and gave one half to Grand Mother Yemaya Mermaid to distribute to the rest of the Old Ems. Then they headed up the Mountains to pay their respects to Bear Woman.

On the way up, the two Old Mermaids feasted on some of the seeds. By the time they reached their destination, they were not feeling as hot and dry as they had been. In fact, they could almost feel the Old Sea coursing through their blood.

As they walked toward Bear Woman's cave, they saw her sitting outside. She did not look like herself. Usually they could not tell if she was Bear or if she was Woman. Today, she was all woman.

"Bear Woman," Sister Ursula Divine Mermaid said. "What ails thee?"

Bear Woman looked up at them. "Hello, Old Mermaids. It is too much for me, methinks. This summer is too difficult. Too little water. Too much sun. Too many deaths. Nothing nourishes me."

Her eyes were milky blue. Her skin was ashy. She usually vibrated power. Now she just seemed exhausted.

The Old Mermaids quickly began pulling sunflower seeds from the half head they had carried up the mountain. Then Sister Ruby Rosarita Mermaid cracked the black shells of some of them between her teeth and handed Bear Woman the meaty centers. Bear Woman popped the seeds into her mouth and began to chew.

After a minute or an hour or a day, her eyes began to shine black again. The sisters blinked and Bear Woman was standing before them, sometimes Bear, sometimes Woman, mostly Bear Woman.

"What took you so long?" Bear Woman growled. "I could have turned into a bunny rabbit. Or a quail."

Sister Ursula Divine Mermaid asked, "Would that have been so bad?"

"Yes!" Bear Woman said. "Because I am not a rabbit or a quail." She opened her mouth and roared. Or growled again. Sisters Ruby Rosarita and Ursula Divine Mermaid did the same. Bear Woman laughed. "That is pathetic. You sound like cubs."

"Compared with you, we are," Sister Ursula Divine Mermaid said.

Bear Woman laughed and laughed. "Who taught the Old Mermaids flattery?"

"It is respect," Sister Ruby Rosarita Mermaid said, "not flattery." She gave Bear Woman another handful of sunflower seeds. Then she and Sister Ursula Divine Mermaid ate some seeds, too.

"We're eating the sun," Bear Woman said, "including all the raw darkness within it. Ain't it grand?"

The Old Mermaids agreed that it was indeed grand.

And then Bear Woman sighed, stood up, and stretched until she was as tall as the tallest tree. The Old Ems wondered for a moment if she was going to go all the way to the sun. But she didn't. She came back to them. "There. I am myself again. Come inside. I saved some berries for you."

So they went into the cave and feasted on sun and berries.

—From *The Old Mermaids Wisdom Cards Guidebook.*

Day Seven:

Sister Bridget Mermaid

October 27

If Sister Bridget Mermaid had a mantra, it would be, "Create, create, create." She brings these to the day:

Suggestion: Sing, dance, create. If you have to choose, do all three at once.

Mystery: Encourage your creative process.

Gift: Poetry and music.

Goddesses

Brigid is an important goddess of pre-Christian Ireland. Like Aine, she is part of the Tuatha Dé Danann. While The Cailleach rules the six months of darkness, Brigid comes out on May 1 to rule over the six months of light (although her feast day is February 1). She is the goddess of smithcraft, poetry, and healing, and she is guardian of the wells. She does it all.

Protection

Do everything you have been doing (grounding, centering, donning the Old Mermaids Suit, taking gems with you). Today ask Brigid to co-create with you a protected healing day.

Cauldron Bubble: What's to Eat or Drink?

The Christian food for St. Brigid was pancakes and cakes. She could turn water into ale and stones into salt. Flour yielded more bread and churning yielded more butter on her celebratory days. Celebrate in any way that feels good to you. It's always lovely to have an excuse to make cake.

Dreams are Made of This

Let your dreams in. Let them show and tell you whatever it is they need to show and tell you.

Altering the Altar

Add water and light to your altar to honor Brigid.

Honoring the Ancestors

Talk to the Dead today. Try not to be boring. You can use Sister Bridget Mermaid's examples of creating a blessing for your dear departed ancestors (see "Charmed, I'm Sure").

Spooky is as Spooky Does

If you're having people over, you can practice psychometry. Ask everyone to bring an object with them, something that has history, preferably unusual history.

Then sit in a circle, quietly. It's more fun to do this in the near dark. Maybe have one candle in the middle. Everyone ground and breathe together for a bit. Start wherever you want. Have one person place in the hand of another person the object they brought. The receiver closes their eyes and meditates on the object. Then the receiver says out loud what they are seeing or hearing or what tale is unfolding to them. The giver tells the receiver when they are correct with a simple "yes" or "that's correct." They don't give any "no" answers. When the receiver is finished, they can give the object to the person next to them and go around circle or you can just do one receiver and one giver for each object. Afterward, you can talk about the process—and who got it right.

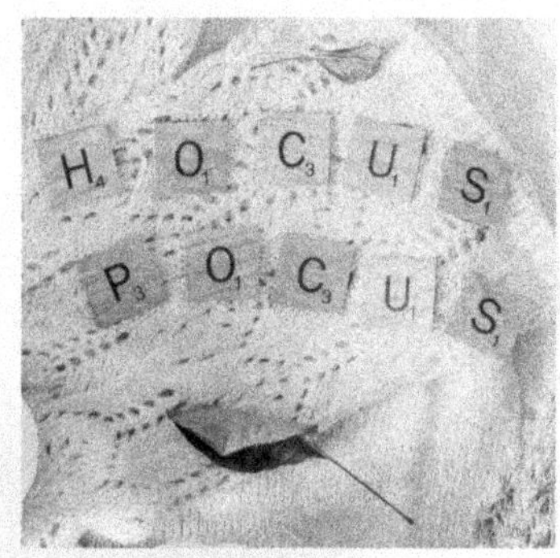

Charmed, I'm Sure

This is one of Sister Bridget Mermaid's charms from *The Old Mermaids Wisdom Cards Guidebook*. Remember, you can call on her or the goddess Brigid when you need inspiration for your creativity.

Charm for Inspiration

Find solace in your works of art.

Find fire in your works of art.

Find adventure in your works of art.

Find shelter in your works of art.

Find rest in your works of art.

Find wisdom in your works of art.

Samhain Symbols

Halloween is often associated with the devil in the minds of some. On Halloween, pitchforks are depicted as part of the costume of the devil. In reality, the pitchfork is something used by country folk in every day life as they fed their livestock and did other chores around the farm. The pitchfork was also seen as a male fertility symbol. Poseidon and Neptune carried the trident. The trident is the alchemical sign for water. Kali's spouse, Shiva, carried the trident. Instead of thinking of it as a symbol of the devil, we can think of it as a phallic symbol of the

mer-gods.

Tales Told

In the summer, the Old Mermaids left the Old Mermaids Sanctuary during the Hottest Days. Like many of their neighbors, they traveled up the mountains before the desert got too hot. They spent their days and nights near their neighbors, amongst the fir trees, near Summit Spring. At night, they sometimes gathered at a small meadow to watch the stars and listen to the owls.

During these days and nights, Sister Bridget Mermaid

planned their Blessing Dance. That's what she called it. The other Old Ems thought of it as Sister Bridget Mermaid's Blessing Time. Because it went on for days—beautiful, lovely days.

Several days (and nights) before the Full Moon, Sister Bridget Mermaid would begin her blessings tour. At sunrise, often after they sang up the Sun, Sister Bridget Mermaid would stand with her palms up and out, facing the Old Mermaids, and say something like, "May the love and affection of the Sun be on you. May the love and affection of these fir trees be on you. May the love and affection of the Old Owl be on you. May the love and affection of the dragonfly be on you. May the love and affection of this mountain be on you. May the love and affection of the New Desert be on you. May my love and affection be on you. All the days and nights for now and forever."

Sister Magdelene Mermaid or maybe Sister DeeDee Lightful

Mermaid would say something like, "Ahhh, it's like beginning the day with spindrift in your wake. Lovely."

At night, before the stars came out, Sister Bridget Mermaid might say something like, "May the power of the stars be yours. May the power of great dreams be yours. May the depth of the trees be yours. May the peace of the mountain nights be yours. May the power of the great bear be yours. May the perspective of the eagle be yours. May all the protection in the world be yours."

Sometimes at midday Sister Bridget Mermaid would have a blessing for them. The neighbors came from far and wide to sit on the ground, close their eyes, and let the blessings flow.

"May the love and affection of the hummingbirds be yours," Sister Bridget Mermaid said. "May the love and affection of the poppies be yours. May the love and affection of the bobcats be yours. May the love and affection of the faeries be yours. May the love and affection of all the Old Mermaids be yours."

But everyone's favorite blessing was the Old Sea Blessing. It was a blessing that had been handed down through time, from mother to daughter, from mother to son, from father to daughter and father to son, forever, although some of the words were changed to fit the place and time.

One year on a late afternoon before the Full Moon rose, Sister Bridget Mermaid stood before the Old Mermaids and the neighbors. She took a deep breath and then let it out, loudly. And then she said, "The Old Sea and the New Desert send to you the deepest blessings to sooth every aching heart and every weary bone.

"The New Desert sends the songs of a mockingbird to you.

"The Old Sea sends a summer shower to you.

"The Old Sea sends the winds from the east to you.

"The New Desert sends the winds from the south to you.

"The Old Sea sends the winds from the west to you.

"The Old Sea sends the winds of the north to you.

"The New Desert sends the healing red of the penstemon to you.

"The New Desert sends the healing black of the crow to you.

"The New Desert sends the healing green of the palo verde to you.

"The Old Sea sends the healing blue of the sky to you!

"The Old Sea sends the peace of flowing streams to you.

"The Old Sea sends the peace of the cooling breezes to you.

"The New Desert sends the peace of the quiet mountain to you.

"The Old Sea sends the peace of the stars, moon, and sun to you.

"Great abiding peace of the Old Mermaids, the New Desert, and the Old Sea to you.

"The Old Sea and the New Desert send you this and more. Love, love, love."

They all stayed in silence for a time, until the Old Owl interrupted or maybe a child sneezed or laughed, and then the blessings began in earnest.

Nearly everyone stood and began showering blessings and gratitude onto everyone else, including the trees, bees, and fleas. It was a love fest that went on and on. When the Full Moon came up and turned its light on the Meadow, the group began to dance and sing. They held hands and wandered the meadow performing the Water Dance, usually with Sister Bridget Mermaid in the lead, their dance becoming the model for the water to follow, to fill up streams, catchments, tinajas, arroyos.

Soon enough, it would be time to come off the mountain, to prepare for the monsoons. The Old Mermaids and neighbors always brought back with them hearts and souls full of Old Mermaids and New Desert blessings.

—From The Old Mermaids Mystery School.

Day Eight:

Sister Ruby Rosarita Mermaid

October 28

Sister Ruby Rosarita Mermaid encourages us to nourish ourselves and make magic every day.

She brings these to the day:

Suggestion: A good bean is hard to find. Everything else is easy.

Mystery: Make magic.

Gift: Enough to eat.

Goddesses

Hecate has a rich and complicated history. For us today, she is the goddess at the crossroads, i.e. the Trivia, and she represents the witch: the powerful woman who reminds us that the everyday actions in our life matter. We are important. Cooking is important. Growing food is important. Delivering babies is important. Even though the monotheistic religions did everything to demonize women—especially independent and elderly women—we are taking back our power and our ability to flourish while doing the

deeds of the Trivia.

Protection

Do your grounding and centering and put on your Old Mermaids protection suit. Consider eating some protective food with intention. Have a bit of salt, maybe some rosemary. All food can be protective as long as you eat it with intention and attention.

Cauldron Bubble: What's to Eat or Drink?

See what your energy level is like. Are you planning a feast for Hallows? If so, another feast today might be too much. Have a good home cooked meal if you can when you do the Dumb Supper. Make certain there is enough protein even if you don't eat meat. Have solid earthy foods like rice, potatoes, carrots, etc.

Dreams are Made of This

Dream of food if you can. What does the dream mean to you?

Altering the Altar

Begin putting photographs and mementoes of the dead on your
altar.

Honoring the Ancestors

The Dumb Supper may be an ancient tradition or a contemporary one. It was (and is) custom to set a place at the Hallows dinner table for the Beloved Dead. Some communities took this custom further by dining in silence with the Dead (thus the "dumb" supper). I will outline a true dumb supper. This is an extremely sacred ritual that you can do now or wait until October 30 or 31.

Plan some kind of dinner. Make it special, even a feast if you like. You can honor one of the Dead or all of them. Different people have different customs. Some say one must have black napkins and black candles and you must drape the deceased's chair in black. I don't think any of that is necessary, but you may want to do it. The Dumb Supper should be reserved for adults— or at least those who can eat in silence. Make certain everyone understands the dinner is in complete silence.

Cleanse and purify the space before dinner and before setting the table. State your intention to honor the dead with this meal. When putting out the place settings, reserve one for the dead. Leave the chair empty, of course. Have guests come in one at a time and give them a chance to stop at the chair of the Dead to say a silent prayer. After everyone is seated, hold hands if you wish and say a silent prayer together. Then serve everyone— including the dead—and eat in silence. Afterward, everyone can leave one at a time and stop at the chair again. Once everyone is out of the room, you can open the circle and then people can come back in and clean up and share experiences.

You can do this yourself, by the way. It is very solemn whether it is you and the Dead or you and a group and the Dead. It's very powerful either way.

Spooky is as Spooky Does

After your Dumb Supper, it's time to pull out your divination tools. Use the tarot cards, the Old Mermaids Wisdom Cards, or a OUIJA board. Talk to the Dead. Ask if they have anything to say to you and then pull a card or use the board. You never know what might happen.

Samhain Symbols

Pointed or conical hats have been around in various cultures for a long while. They were popular in India at one time. Jewish people were forced to wear identifying pointed hats in medieval Europe. The pope wore (and wears) a tall hat—although it's not exactly pointed. Two female mummies in China dating from the fourth and second centuries BCE were discovered with tall pointed hats. The Tarim mummies wore pointed hats as well. The priestess mummies in Siberia also had tall pointed hats.

There's a portrait from 1676 hanging in the Tate of a woman with her grandchildren, and she is wearing what we would call a witch's hat. I've read some theories that pointed hats—like a "dunce cap"—were used to strengthen one's mind or power.

Pointed hats were worn by gods, too. According to Barbara Walker, during the Inquisition when the church was trying to kill off "heretics," they targeted people with pointed hats and diminished their power by putting the pointed hats on people who weren't very smart. I don't know what the truth is. I do know I like wearing my witch's hat. I feel linked to my sisters and mothers and grandmothers through time.

Tales Told

"I went out to the crossroads once," Sister Ruby Rosarita Mermaid said, "after the Witch of Coyote Hill said lots of scary things happen at the crossroads."

"Was it scary?" Sister Laughs A Lot Mermaid asked.

"A young man with a guitar by his side was the first to arrive as the moon rose over the mountains," Sister Ruby Rosarita Mermaid said. "He was so skinny, and he looked more tired than any of us has ever been."

"Oh, I know this tale," the Witch said. "Did he think you were the devil?"

"He did!" Sister Ruby Rosarita Mermaid said. "He said, 'Are you the devil? I have come to sell my soul for success with my music. I need success so that I have money to eat, to walk, to sleep. My soul ain't worth nothing here.'

"I said, 'I don't know what a devil is, so I can't buy your soul or make you a success.'

"He sank to the ground with his guitar next to him. I swear a wind would have blown him away had there been one. I told him I could make him something to eat. And right then and there a kitchen appeared all around me, and I cooked this boy eggs and potatoes and soup and salad and bread with butter and a big pot of stew. Just like that." She snapped her fingers. "He ate everything I gave him. When he was finished, he stood, took his guitar out, and played me the most beautiful song I have ever heard. And I told him so. He shook his head. 'It's not good enough. But I thank you for the meal. It's the best I have ever had. I'll head down to the next crossroads. Maybe I'll find the devil there. Or someone who will buy these magic beans I have.'

"Then he disappeared into the darkness. The Witch was right that the crossroads are a scary place. Saddest and scariest thing I have ever seen: Someone who did not know how beautiful and talented he was."

Day Nine:

Sister Sophia Mermaid

October 29

Sister Sophia Mermaid wants you to use your wisdom—and go with the flow.

She brings these to the day:

Suggestion: Go with the flow—and watch out for waterfalls.

Mystery: Be wise.

Gift: Wisdom.

Goddesses

Eriskegal is the Great Sumerian Goddess of the Underworld, which she rules. Her sister Inanna is the ruler of the Heavens and the Earth. Eriskegal is all-knowing, like Sophia. And she demands the truth. She is who you can call on when you are in a depression. She will gnash her teeth, pull out her hair, and scream until you face the truth. (She figures in my novel *The Jigsaw Woman* and in my short book *MommaEarth Goddess Runes*.) She is so powerful because she will not suffer fools, even if that fool is you.

Protection

You know what to do.

Cauldron Bubble: What's to Eat or Drink?

What would you eat if you were trapped in the Underworld? A pomegranate? Eat something full of natural color and vitality, so you can enliven yourself out of the Underworld.

Dreams are Made of This

You are probably dreaming on your own now. Don't do anything to interrupt the flow. If you aren't dreaming, consider getting off screens for an hour or so before you sleep. Don't have coffee or any caffeine before bed, of course. Allow yourself to get sleepy before going to bed. Keep pen and paper by the bed to record any dreams immediately upon waking.

Altering the Altar

Continue displaying photos of the dead on your altar. You can use photos from magazines and other places to display animals who are no longer on the planet. How can you honor the Underworld with your altar?

Honoring the Ancestors

Honor your ancestors by being wise today: Take good care of yourself.

Spooky is as Spooky Does

Do you have any spookiness where you live? Is your house haunted? Does a poltergeist live in your closet? Allow yourself to explore these possibilities without opening the door all the way. Protect yourself and your space and ask very respectfully if anyone else lives there with you. Only do this if you are prepared for the truth.

Samhain Symbols

The broomstick—or besom—has long been associated with women. According to Barbara Walker, in Rome sacred midwives used special brooms to sweep clear the thresholds of households after a baby was born. The broom was sometimes called the faery horse, and Medieval inquisitors accused "witches" of riding their brooms to naked dances in the woods—or anywhere the witches could cause trouble. Actually "riding the broom" can be seen as a shamanic act. The shaman or medicine woman rides the drum or the broom to connect with the spirit world to do her healing magic. A homemade broom is a lovely instrument to use to magically clear a space. You sweep as usual but with intention to clear out anything that can cause harm or doesn't belong in the space.

Tales Told

Sister Sophia Mermaid found a cave on her way down from

visiting the Old Woman and Old Man of the Mountains one day.

She wasn't sure if it was the wise thing to do, but she went

inside the darkness, lit a candle, and continued walking.

She walked until she heard, "Who goes there?"

She took a few more steps and the narrow passageway

opened up. A woman the color of the green slime that covered the cave walls (for some unknown reason) was bent over a cauldron in the middle of the cave. Fire licked the black sides.

"Who are you?" the green slime woman screamed.

"I am Sister Sophia Mermaid," she said.

"I didn't call you," the woman screamed. "Why are you here? Don't you know I will tear your head off?"

Sister Sophia Mermaid shrugged. "I've already lost my tails and my home and my world. Not sure losing my head would change anything."

The woman looked up at her. "I am Eriskegal, goddess of the Underworld. Don't you know me?"

"I do not," Sister Sophia Mermaid said, "but I would be glad to know you."

Eriskegal sat on a stone bench near the cauldron. She waved to another stone bench and Sister Sophia Mermaid sat on it.

"Is this the Underworld?" Sister Sophia Mermaid asked.

Eriskegal roared with laughter. "No. I'm not sure what this place is. I was wandering and ended up here."

"Perhaps you needed sanctuary," Sister Sophia Mermaid said.

"Me? The goddess of death and destruction? Why would I need sanctuary?"

"Maybe you are tired of your routine," Sister Sophia Mermaid said.

Eriskegal laughed. "I am tired of the morons who stumble into my realm. Not a one them understands what truth is. Not a one of them has their heads out of their asses."

"Sounds like they have more than one head and more than one ass."

Eriskegal chuckled. "They don't understand reality."

"Do you?"

Eriskegal stared at Sister Sophia Mermaid quietly for a

moment. Then she sighed. "We are born, we live, we die. What more?"

"Everything in-between is what more."

"They don't realize how short it all is," Eriskegal said. "They live their short stupid lives while I am stuck in the Underworld where I have to deal with their foolishness."

"You help them discover the truth," Sister Sophia Mermaid said. "Don't you? Or maybe they visit your realm to show you the truth. Each of them may carry a gem of truth for you."

"I hadn't thought of it that way," Eriskegal said. "Perhaps I should not slay them so quickly in the future. I will listen to what they have to say first."

Sister Sophia Mermaid laughed.

"What is funny?" the mistress of death asked.

"Um, nothing. Except: You actually slay them?"

Eriskegal nodded. "I think it's all metaphor. You know, they descend to the Underworld without all of their trappings from the outer world so they can face their true selves—including their death. Then they can ascend into the world again and live their authentic lives. Blah, blah, blah."

"Do you know your true self?" Sister Sophia Mermaid asked.

"I think my true self is actually a beach bum," Eriskegal said. "Without a care in the world."

"It sounds like you need a vacation," Sister Sophia Mermaid said. "I think I know just the place."

"Is it a sunny beach?"

"It is sunny," Sister Sophia Mermaid said, "and it used to be an ocean, so I guess now it's all beach. It's called the Old Mermaids Sanctuary."

"It sounds like a place where you are all delusional," Eriskegal said.

Sister Sophia Mermaid laughed. "No, not at all. It's just that everyone needs a break from death and destruction now and again."

"All right," Eriskegal said. "I will take a vacay."

They began walking out of the cave.

"And no slaying for a while," Sister Sophia Mermaid said.

"Even if someone pisses me off?" Eriskegal asked.

"Even then."

Day Ten:

Sister Magdelene Mermaid

October 30

Sister Magdelene Mermaid is the heart of the Old Mermaids

Sanctuary in many ways because she is the embodiment of love.

She brings these to the day:

Suggestion: You ask me to tell you about love. Showing is so

much better.

Mystery: Love.

Gift: Love.

Goddesses

When Europeans converted to Christianity (often unwillingly), they did not give up their goddesses easily. As Patricia Monaghan writes in *Goddesses and Heroines*, "What Christianity denied was the possibility of divine femininity. . . . Christianity provided no image of the mother goddess to substitute for the ones they revered so highly."

After a time, the converted Pagans found Mary. She was split into the virgin and the whore by the church, just as Tonantzin was in the Americas when the Spanish colonized the land and the religion of the native people there.

The herstory of Mary Magdalene is complicated. Books have been written about her. Was she a rich woman following Jesus? Was she a prostitute who became Jesus' companion and convert? Did Jesus and Mary Magdalene marry? Some scholars link her with the Black Madonna and call her an Ethiopian priestess for Isis. Or was she Isis, powerful goddess of Egypt and wife of the king of the dead? This would link the folklore of Jesus with the dark goddess. Was he then a follower of hers?

These are all interesting ideas to contemplate.

Protection

Ground and connect. Take your gemstones with you. Perhaps add a heart to your pocket today in honor of Sister Magdelene Mermaid.

Cauldron Bubble: What's to Eat or Drink?

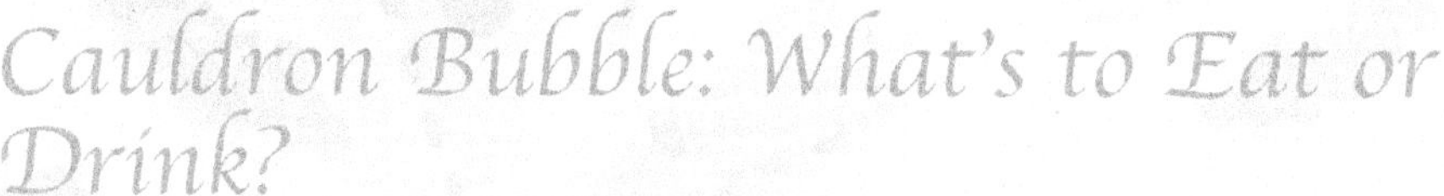

Have some love apples today in honor of Mary Magdalene and her aspect as Aphrodite, i.e. tomatoes. Apparently the French believe tomatoes are aphrodisiacs.

Plan your Hallows or Day of the Dead feast and make certain you have all the ingredients you need.

Dreams are Made of This

If you have been having vivid dreams, now might be time to ask for a lucid dream. Before falling asleep, tell yourself, "In my next dream, I want to know I'm dreaming." Say this over and over as you go into slumberland.

Altering the Altar

Continue putting photos of your ancestors or anyone else who has died on your altar. Add photos or drawings of animals, plants, etc. that have gone extinct.

Honoring the Ancestors

Write a poem or letter to a dead ancestor. No one else has to ever see it, so don't worry if it's not perfect. Think of it as a love poem. Say all the things you wish you had been able to say when they were alive. Or choose an ancestor you never knew and tell them how much you appreciate them surviving so that you could live.

This is my love letter to my ancestors:

O My Ancestors

O my Ancestors

Upon your ashes I walk through life

Upon your dust I shall one day rest

O my Ancestors

You who flew above the Earth

You who burned with Passion

You who made your home in the Ocean

You who burrowed deep into the Earth

O my Ancestors

I ask for your blessings

And thank you for my life

Ashes to ashes

Dust to dust

All my relations

O my Ancestors

Spooky is as Spooky Does

If you detected a spirit in your house, ask for a benign but clear sign that they are really there. Give a time limit. "If you could please give me a benign and evident sign that you are here by 6 p.m. " See if it works.

Charmed, I'm Sure

Here is a purification charm. I originally used it in *The Salmon Mysteries*, and I called on Demeter and Persephone, but you can call on any god or goddess, the Universe, your Higher Self, or your ancestors. Have water with you. Here I call upon Mary Magdalene.

Charm to Call Mary Magdalene

With this sacred water

Mary Magdalene, priestess of love

With this sacred water

Purify and heal me.

I am Mother, I am Daughter,

Lover of all I see:

Sky, mountain, river, and field

Mother/Daughter, blessed me!

Give me power I can wield.

Purify and heal me, blessed be.

Tales Told

One night during Dark Moon, Sister Magdelene Mermaid walked through the wash. A breeze rustled through the dry hackberry bushes, pencil cholla, and mesquite. A Tall Dark Figure stopped a short distance from the Old Em.

"This will be the path of the Wild Hunt," Tall Dark Figure said. "Why are you here?"

"I prepare the path with my love, " Sister Magdelene Mermaid said.

"This is the Wild Hunt," Tall Dark Figure said, the disgust not disguised in their voice. "Love has no place here. Don't you know the world is filled with evil and destruction and horror?"

"Love has a place everywhere," she said. "You think I don't understand the world because I still love? You are wrong. I still love because I understand the world. It's not a puppy love, although I do love puppies and I suppose that is actually puppy love. But my love is an action, it is a devotion. It means I stand for the world. Including those who have died. Haven't you ever loved?"

"Of course not! And any of the participants in the wild hunt could tear you to bits and take you to the Underworld with them," Tall Dark Figure said. "Does that not frighten you?"

"Sometimes," Sister Magdelene Mermaid said. "And sometimes it doesn't."

"What is that in your hand?" Tall Dark Figure asked. "It is light. We need no light at this time."

"It is stardust," Sister Magdelene Mermaid said, and she let some of it sprinkle down from her finger tips. Each particle seemed to pick up light from who knows where: the stars above, Sister Magdelene Mermaid's eyes. "We are all made from it, even you, Tall Dark Figure."

"I eat stardust for lunch," Tall Dark Figure said, "and poop out universes by dinner."

"That is quite a skill," Sister Magdelene Mermaid said. She held out her stardust-filled hands. "Would you like some now, tonight, so you can poop out more universes by morning?"

"You are a cheeky Old Em," Tall Dark Figure said. "If you are all so fearless, maybe you will survive the Wild Hunt, should you stumble into it."

"We are all different," Sister Magdelene Mermaid said.

"I don't have time for any more stardust talk."

"OK," Sister Magdelene Mermaid said. "If I see you during the Wild Hunt, I'll wave and say hello."

"We don't wave and say hello during the Wild Hunt," they said, sounding exasperated.

"What do you do then?"

"We are a horde of ravishers looking for souls to take," they said. "We don't wave. We don't say hello."

Sister Magdelene Mermaid laughed. "I will take note of that. But I may forget and wave anyway."

"Then you'll just draw attention to yourself and someone will snatch your soul."

"That doesn't sound fun," she said. "All right. I will take your advice. No waving or saying hello."

"It is not advice," they said. "I don't give advice." They shook their head. Then they walked by her in the wash. Their passing created a little breeze, and stardust wafted out of Sister Magdelene Mermaid's hands.

"Oh, it looks so beautiful on your black robes," Sister Magdelene Mermaid said.

"I am not beautiful!" they said as they kept walking. "Just stay hidden during it all."

"More advice!" Sister Magdelene Mermaid called. "You do love me!"

"I do not," they said. "I do not, I do not, I do—" and they disappeared into the night.

Sister Magdelene Mermaid smiled. "What a grumpy destructive goose," she said as she continued walking and letting loose stardust from her fingertips. "I wonder what one wears to a Wild Hunt?"

Grand Mother Yemaya Mermaid

October 31

Happy Halloween!

Grand Mother Yemaya Mermaid knows all, and she encourages us to go with the flow no matter what is happening. She is the dark grand mother rising up from the waters for all to see. She is connected to the great Yoruba Mother Ocean goddess.

Goddess Yemaya rules everything that has to do with women; therefore, she rules all and is known and worshipped around the planet.

Grand Mother Yemaya Mermaid brings these to the day:

Suggestion: Laugh or weep. We swim in your tears.

Mystery: Flow.

Gift: Mysteries of the Old Sea.

Goddesses

This is the time of The Cailleach, the Morrigan, the Sheela Na Gigs. They act as the Bone Mother or they are the Bone Mother.

The Bone Mother is the one who gathers the bones from the forest, the desert, the riverside, and sings them back to life. She is the shaman, the medicine woman, the bone mother, the psychopomp: She heals and she escorts the souls to the land of the dead or to Summerland.

The Wild Hunt is when the goddess of the Underworld is hunting for bones of the dead. She comes when the veil is thin, usually with a consort. She is at the head of the Cavalcade of Spirits looking for souls of the dead to psychopomp, to take them home to the Underworld. On this night of the Wild Hunt, anything left in the fields (after Samhain) belonged to the fairies. On this night, too, the good battled the bad. In Italy, for instance, the benandanti would "fly" in the night to fight the malandenti, the bad spirits.

Essentially this is about the witches or shamans or medicine people or benandanti—whatever name they called themselves— going into trances in order to protect their communities from bad spirits who might spoil their crops or make them sick and to take "home" the souls of the dead who might be wandering.

The members of the Wild Hunt were the spirit clean-up crew to clear the decks for the new year.

What we can do ourselves on the night of the Wild Hunt is to leave out food or other sustenance for the benandanti and wish them well.

Protection

Make certain you ground. Put on your Old Mermaids protection suit. Carry protective stones with you for the next three days. Eat well, sleep well, drink water.

Today is a good day to decide to let go of what does not serve you. You can make a list of what isn't working for you, decide to let it go, and then burn the list or tear it into bits. Then think about what you would like to bring into the new year. Being aware of what isn't good for you and what isn't working and taking steps to change these things is the best protection you can give yourself.

Cauldron Bubble: What's to Eat or Drink?

If you are celebrating October 31 as Samhain, as New Year's Eve, you might want to have a feast. We often have the equivalent of a Thanksgiving meal on this evening. Or sometimes we make lasagne or something else that feels very hearty to eat. We often make luna cookies, too. It's basically a sugar cookie recipe that we shape into full moons or crescent moons. You are celebrating the old year and welcoming in the new.

I recommend including apples in your meal or feast.

And if you are having a Dumb Supper now, leave an empty chair and place setting to represent the dead at your table. You can decide to have the entire meal in silence or not. It's up to you. What is important is to honor those who have gone before us.

Dreams are Made of This

I am hoping you are beginning to have dreams from your beloved dead. May it be healing for you.

Altering the Altar

Now is the time to put the finishing touches on your altar. Represent your human ancestors on the altar. You might also want to represent the flora and fauna that carry stardust in their bodies, too. Think about adding something for each of the four elements: earth, air, fire, and water. Some people add a fifth element: spirit/ether/space.

Research your own heritage to see if you can determine how your ancestors may have created altars or sacred spaces.

I happen to have a little black Samhain tree that I decorate with little ornaments that represent the season. They are funny, and they are solemn. I don't have a lot of photos of people I've loved and lost, so I often write their names on small pieces of paper or put a thing on the altar that represents them to me, like something they gave me or something that reminds me of them.

When it feels finished, bless it. Come up with your own prayer or chant. Could be something like this:

Chant to Bless the Altar

On this night when spirits roam,

Ancestors, we invite you home.

Know we love you all year long.

Tonight this is where you belong.

No pressure, no demands,

Only love throughout the lands.

We intend no harm.

Let there only be good charm.

Honoring the Ancestors

This entire day is about honoring the ancestors: creating (or finishing) the altar and having a Dumb Supper or leaving a plate for the ancestors.

Spooky is as Spooky Does

This is a good day for ghost stories. It's also a proper time to go out to the crossroads (or the end of your driveway), and leave an offering for Hecate or someone else. Since I live where wild things roam, I don't do this any more. I don't want to give the critters people food because they shouldn't have people food. It's not good for them. So often, I go out to the crossroads and say a prayer or chant of appreciation.

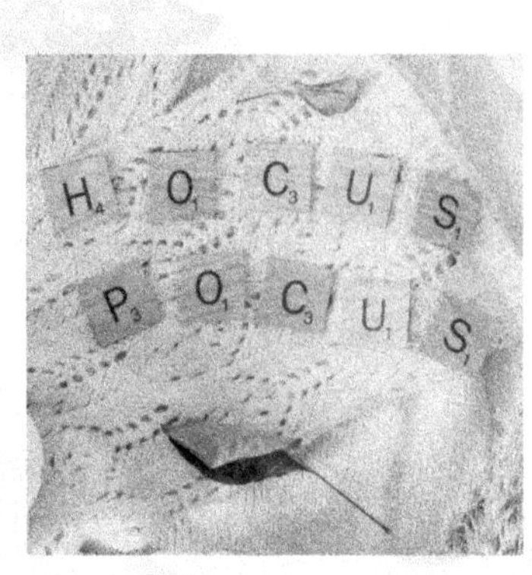

Charmed, I'm Sure

Charm for the Living and the Dead

As you carry on, may peace be on you

Wherever you be, may peace be on you

Whoever you are now and then

May peace be on you

All the days and nights of life

All the days and nights of death.

Samhain Symbols

In North America and much of Europe, apples were harvested now. They were part of the last harvest that is Samhain. Samhain is the Festival of Apples, after all. Apples were seen as the food of the dead. If you had an apple bough that had buds on it, you would be able to enter the Underworld with it.

Cut an apple in half, horizontally, and you'll find a five pointed star. Now that is magic.

Tales Told

Once the Old Mermaids came to the New Desert, they all became Bone Mothers of one sort or another. They picked up bones and branches and lost dreams and sang them back to life or helped them find the way to Summerland.

So it made sense that when any of the Old Neighbors discovered a pile of bones, they brought the bones to the Old Mermaids or brought the Old Mermaids to the bones. This happened late one night or early one morning when the Old

Mermaids followed Old Neighbor Louie into the wash. They walked a long while until they saw Betty, the Woman Who Weaves, waiting for them. The sun came up over the ridge just then, spreading sweet light across the desert, creating a gold and red halo around everything. The Old Mermaids went to Betty and looked at what lay at her feet.

They were the bones of an Old Mermaid.

Grand Mother Yemaya Mermaid and Mother Star Stupendous Mermaid thanked Louie and Betty. The Old Neighbors nodded and then left the Old Mermaids alone.

"I wonder who," Sister Laughs A Lot Mermaid said.

"When?" Sister Magdelene Mermaid asked.

"When the Old Sea dried up," Sister Sophia Mermaid said. "When else?"

"What should we do?" Sister Lyra Musica Mermaid asked.

"Take her back," Sister Faye Mermaid said. "Back to the Old Sea."

"If we could do that," Sister Bea Wilder Mermaid said, "we'd take ourselves back." The Old Mermaids were silent. "Wouldn't we?"

"They say the Big River flows into what's left of the Old Sea," Grand Mother Yemaya Mermaid said. "Let's take her there."

The other Old Mermaids agreed. Grand Mother Yemaya Mermaid unfolded the quilt she had carried under her arm and she laid it on the desert floor. The others carefully picked up the bones of the Old Mermaid and put them on the comforter. Grand Mother Yemaya Mermaid folded the cloth up around the bones. Then she lifted the bundle into her arms. The Old Mermaids began walking. Sister Bridget Mermaid and Sister Faye Mermaid started singing sea chanties, and soon the others joined it. Then they started the encouragements: "You'll be home soon, Sister Mermaid."

"Oh, you'll be in the Old Sea in no time."

"Say hello to everyone for us."

"It'll be a grand time."

And then they sang some more.

When they reached the shores of the Big River, it was near night. Grand Mother Yemaya Mermaid stepped forward, a bit away from the other Old Mermaids, and looked down at the rushing water. The Old Mermaids sang softly near her. Grand Mother Yemaya Mermaid said, "May you be, may you be, may you be," and she slowly began unwrapping the quilt.

I can't be sure of what happened next. I can only tell you what was told to me. As she unwrapped the quilt to drop the bones of the Old Mermaid into the river, the bones slipped away on their own. Only they weren't bones. Some say a salmon twisted out of the quilt and leaped into the water. Some say a faery slid away. Still others say it was the Old Mermaid herself, restored to life. The Old Mermaids didn't know what happened. It was dark. Grand Mother Yemaya Mermaid was so startled, she dropped the quilt. It fell right into the river and disappeared along with the salmon or the faery or the New Old Mermaid.

One or more of the Old Mermaids swore they heard, "I'm goin' home, sisters!" coming from the water.

The Old Mermaids began clapping and cheering and laughing and dancing in the moonlight and river light. Everyone says that you could see their tails flashing like a thousand tiny colored moons. Or gills on a fish. You take your pick.

Sometime later, the Old Mermaids walked home to the Old Mermaids Sanctuary, picking up bones, seashells, and sweet dreams on the way.

Day Twelve:

Mother Star Stupendous Mermaid

November 1

When Mother Star Stupendous Mermaid shows up, it is time to be. Rest on your laurels and see what happens. The stars are not only aligned, they are all around us. Today is the first day of the pagan new year. Relax from your feasting. Perhaps make yourself a list of what you would like to achieve this coming year. Or not.

Remember: you are stardust and Mother Star Stupendous Mermaid loves you.

Mother Star Stupendous Mermaid brings these to the day:

Suggestion: All the wisdom of the ages can be distilled into one suggestion: Be.

Mystery: Honor the ancestors.

Gift: The stars, earth, moon, and sun.

Goddesses

Sometimes trying to figure out the herstory of goddesses makes my head spin. When Mother Star Stupendous Mermaid walked into my imagination, I saw a connection between her and the goddess Astarte. In mythology Astarte became Aphrodite, or the other way around, and was worshipped as Inanna in other places (with Inanna probably being the oldest of them all). For this particular holiday season, Inanna, Queen of Heaven, has a relevant tale for us. She heard the beating of the drum to become something else, to find the truth of her life, and she went down, down, down where the Queen of the Underworld, Inanna's sister Eriskegal, killed her and hung her on a hook for three days until she was rescued.

Inanna returned to the Upper World, but she was never the same. None of us is ever the same once we've made that descent. (My book *The Jigsaw Woman* is all about this journey.) During this time of the year, we often connect deeply with our beloved dead. We will never be the same without them, but we belong here in the Upper World.

Protection

Be here and now even if the spirits are still calling to you. Do all your grounding exercises. Do a short (or long) meditation. Eat solid grounding food. Wear your Old Mermaid suit, of course. And be firm with yourself that this is where you belong.

Cauldron Bubble: What's to Eat or Drink?

Relax. Eat whatever you have on hand: beans, chocolate, eggs, cheese, cake. Not all at once. Don't give yourself a tummy ache.

Dreams are Made of This

Although your ancestors can reach you any time through your dreams, ask for a dream to carry you into the new year. Ask if they could show you one thing that can be a symbol for you to take with you—either figuratively or metaphorically—for the rest of the year.

Altering the Altar

Your altar is fine the way it is.

Honoring the Ancestors

Either today or tomorrow go out to the cemetery. If you have people there, clean up around their graves. Leave them flowers or something they would appreciate. Talk to them.

Spooky is as Spooky Does

Spooky times are over. Celebrate. Be joyful. Remember good times. And if part of those good times was watching a scary movie, go for it.

Charmed, I'm Sure

This is not a charm, really, but a piece from an ancient poem about the passage of Ishtar/Inanna to the Underworld:

Ishtar/Inanna Poem

If you do not open the gate for me to come in,

I shall smash the door and shatter the bolt,

I shall smash the doorpost and overturn the doors,

I shall raise up the dead and they shall eat the living:

And the dead shall outnumber the living!

Tales Told

On this night, the Old Ems all go out and look up at the night sky. They watch with delight as the stars move above them. Sometimes, for a moment or two, one or more of them will feel as though they are floating on the Old Sea again. Then they will realize the Old Sea is long gone. The dead are dead. And the Old Mermaids are alive in the New Desert. They hold hands and listen for the songs of the ancestors, the songs of the stars, the songs of the universe. All the songs start the same and end the same: "Oh my darling dears, you belong here. Oh my darling dears, you belong here."

Day Thirteen:

Sister Faye Mermaid

November 2

Sister Faye Mermaid reminds us of "the fey" and Morgan Le Fay in particular. Fey equals fairy. Morgan Le Fay is seen as a Celtic death goddess, possibly the triple goddess Morrigan. Our Sister Faye Mermaid would be considered an extraordinary witch, sorcerer, shaman, medicine woman, conjurer if she weren't an

Old Mermaid. But then again, all the Old Mermaids could lay claim to those titles if they wished.

Sister Faye Mermaid brings these to the day:

Suggestion: The rest is . . . mystery.

Mystery: Accept mystery.

Gift: Healing and magic.

Goddesses

The Morrigan is an extremely important Celtic goddess, and she takes on many forms. She is part of the Tuatha Dé Danann. Sometimes she is a giant standing by the well to tell the fortunes of those who go into battle. She is a war goddess whose name might mean death queen or great queen.

Mara Freeman in *Kindling the Celtic Spirit* says the Morrigan's name means "phantom queen." She was a battle fury whose screams terrorized the enemies of her people. And her chants and spells could bring on all kinds of enchantments to confuse the

warriors. She was also a goddess of the people and the land.

Protection

You know what to do. And when you take down your altar—if you do—make certain you are protected and grounded.

Cauldron Bubble: What's to Eat or Drink?

If you still feel like feasting, feast away. Otherwise, have some leftovers. Begin to unwind from the 13 day celebration.

In some European countries, people make soul cakes on this day. Originally these were made on All Souls' Day to give away to the poor. Now, they are usually on hand at home in case one has visitors.

For the Day of the Dead festivities, celebrants make Pan de

Muertos (Bread of the Dead). It is placed on the ofrenda and/or eaten at the gravesites. (You can search online for recipes.)

Dreams are Made of This

If you feel like it, look at the dreams you have had over the last 12 nights. Try to determine if there is a narrative or a repeat of certain items or themes. Determine if there is an overall message that may help you in the New Year.

Altering the Altar

You can leave the altar for another day or you can start

disassembling it, unless you are keeping it up for the year.

Remember if you took anything from Nature that needs putting

back and then put it back.

Honoring the Ancestors

As you take apart the altar, talk to your ancestors and thank them for your life. If you are celebrating at their gravesite, you are also honoring them.

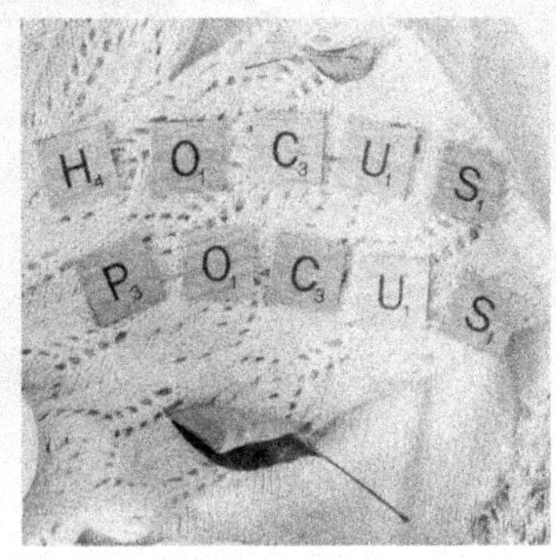

Charmed, I'm Sure

Charm to Say Goodbye to Our Ancestors.

Peace of the morning sun be on you.

Peace of a baby's smile be on you.

Strength of the Old Oak on you.

Perspective of the Old Vulture on you.

Love of your descendants on you

For now and forever.

Samhain Symbols

Marigolds are not a Samhain symbol, but they certainly remind me of this holiday season. Marigolds are a part of the Dia de los Muertos celebrations. I've heard many reasons for this. One, they're a bright-colored flower and this is a celebration, after all. Having marigolds on the altar helps guide the dead to the altar because they are so bright-colored and pungent. One source said they are important for this time of the year because they grow in the woods—and they are everywhere in bloom now where I live in the Southwest. They were used medicinally and considered sacred to the Aztecs, apparently, and they bred them to be bigger and brighter.

Tales Told

The Old Mermaids and some of the Old Neighbors stepped into the wash one evening during that time when the ancestors were especially honored. The moon was bright that particular night. Sister Faye Mermaid was at the front of the group as they walked over the sand.

"The time is nigh," she sang, "to say our goodbyes. All our dears, we know you'll stay near."

As she sang, something in the wash shifted, and they could all see the colorful shimmering in the wash. It was as though a translucent curtain hung over the wash.

And just then, the Fairy Queen's white horse stepped down into the wash. The Fairy Queen nodded at the Old Mermaids. Then she and the horse slipped through the curtains, followed by her consort on a black horse, and then the Cavalcade of Spirits that went on and on and on—some were full of light and potential, others were twisted and distorted. After a while, people became recognizable just before they stepped through the curtain.

"Look, there's Terry." Waving. "Awww, he saw me, waved. Love you!"

"My old paint. Lovely to see her full of life again."

"I don't see anything."

"Over there." Pointing. "It's your mother. See her?" Waving.

"Yes! Mama! Here I am."

"No. You can't go to her. Stay."

"So many . . ."

Sister Laughs A Lot Mermaid giggled.

Sister Lyra Musica Mermaid whispered to the Old Mermaids. "I don't see anything."

"It took me a minute," Sister Ursula Divine Mermaid said. "Squint a bit."

"Listen with your heart," Sister Sheila Na Giggles Mermaid said.

"Can you see anyone we know?" Sister Lyra Musica Mermaid asked.

Sister Magdelene Mermaid said, "Not yet, darlin', not yet."

"I see my Old Old Mermaid," Mother Star Stupendous Mermaid said. "There!" She blew her a kiss.

"Is it the Old Sea?" Sister Lyra Musica Mermaid asked. "Has the Old Sea returned?"

Sister Bea Wilder Mermaid said, "There are so many dolphins, from our old pod!"

"Oh, wisdom breathes all around us," Sister Sophia Mermaid said.

The Old Ems were excited now, too, as their neighbors continued to point out old dead friends.

"I see the coral!" Sister Ruby Rosarita Mermaid said. "Remember how bright it was?"

"The Old Sea, is it there?" Sister Lyra Musica Mermaid asked. She closed her eyes. Was that the sea she smelled? She breathed deeply. Home, home, home.

Was that the sea she heard? The waves? The breath of fishes?

"Yes, dear Sister Lyra, it's the Old Sea," Sister Bridget Mermaid said.

Sister Lyra Musica Mermaid opened her eyes and gasped. The Old Sea was all around them! They were enveloped by it. They were *in* it! They were a part of it again. It moved around them, held them. The creatures of the Old Sea bumped into them as a way of saying hello. The fish. The crabs. The great Old Whale. Life hummed around them.

Home, sweet ever home, sweet home. . . .

Sister Lyra Musica Mermaid sighed with relief and love. The Old Mermaids swam all around her, their tails colorful in so many ways in the water. Her tail! Orange and blue and a part of her. Her tail!

Ahead of them, the curtain undulated, and the curtain pulled them toward it.

Then a cloud went over the moon.

Darkness.

Sister Lyra Musica Mermaid breathed deeply. Moved her arms.

The cloud moved away from the moon.

They were standing in the wash. The curtain was gone. The Old Neighbors were heading home.

"But we were home," Sister Lyra Musica Mermaid whispered.

"We are home, sweetheart," Sister DeeDee Lightful Mermaid said.

Sister Lyra Musica Mermaid wiped the moisture from her face. Was it what was left of the Old Sea or her tears?

"Remember, laugh or weep," Grand Mother Yemaya Mermaid said, "we swim in your tears."

The Old Mermaids started back to the Sanctuary. Sister Lyra Musica Mermaid said, "What happened to the Old Sea?"

"Who knows," someone whispered.

Sister Faye Mermaid put her arm across Sister Lyra Musica Mermaid's shoulders. "The rest is always mystery," she said. "The rest is mystery."

Index

About the Author

Kim Antieau's books include many accounts of the Old Mermaids and their adventures in the Old Sea and the New Desert. Among them are *Church of the Old Mermaids, The Fish Wife,* and *The Blue Tail.* She has also distilled much of the wisdom of the Old Mermaids into several non-fiction books, including *The Old Mermaids Mystery School, The Old Mermaids Book of Days and Nights,* and *The Old Mermaids Oracle.* Kim has also created a divination deck of cards, *The Old Mermaids Wisdom Cards,* along with a guidebook for the deck. Her other books include *The Jigsaw Woman, Whackadoodle Times, Ruby's Imagine, Queendom: Feast of the Saints, The Monster's Daughter, Killing Beauty, Coyote Cowgirl, The Salmon Mysteries,* and *Answering the Creative Call.* She lives in the Southwest with her husband, Mario Milosevic.

More about Kim's writing at her website: kimantieau.com. Kim's photographs are at kimantieau.smugmug.com.